NAUGHTY OR NICE

MALEVOLENT SINNERS

SAMANTHA BARRETT

Oh sinner...
You dirty little whore, you knew this series would be
just as sinful as the first, and you still dared to pick up
this one-handed read without remorse.
What a good fucking slut you are!
Now, charge those batteries and get that clit ready to be
serviced because I'm about to fuck you raw with
this one...

CHAPTER ONE

HOLLY

> Chester - I can't do this anymore.
> Find someone else. I have.

I've read the message at least a dozen fucking times, and still my anger hasn't lessened. I am fucking furious.

I gave that sorry ass excuse of a fucking man everything. I let him slip his needle-sized dick inside me and faked orgasm after orgasm just so his ego wouldn't be wounded, and he had the audacity to fuck me over!

I inhale through my nose and try to push my anger down. I have a function tonight and I can't let my boss down. Nick gave me a shot when no one else in New York City would. I had no experience or a degree, but he didn't care. He said I had heart, and that's all that matters. I give myself another second to wallow in my anger. When the elevator dings, announcing my arrival, I plaster a fake ass smile on my face just as the doors open and the sound of music assaults me.

I fight not to cringe at the Christmas music blasting around me. Everyone is dressed up in their best costumes for the party but I just wasn't feeling it so I went with a red sequin dress that hugs my curves in all the right places and makes me feel like a badass bitch. I feel so fucking sexy right now, I would be open to trying *Nyotaimori*.

I stick to the outskirts of the room and try to go unnoticed by everyone but I can't shake the feeling I'm being watched.

I discreetly look around the room but everyone seems to be either conversing, dancing or sipping on a drink and not paying me any attention at all. I purse my lips and try to shake off the feeling of being watched as I order a couple of shots from the bar and a gin and tonic to chase the burn of the Fireball shots away. I plan on getting wasted and forgetting what the fuck my name is. Chester was a fucking douchebag but I can't lie and say him dropping me like a sack of shit doesn't sting.

I slam the first shot and relish the burn as it slides down my throat, the second goes down as easy as a cock would slide inside my tight, wet cunt right now. I chase them with my gin and tonic before ordering another round of the same. I'm feeling warm and slightly buzzed, a few more rounds of these and I'll forget all about that fucking piece of shit.

I lift the shot to my lips, down the contents, then pause when I get that sensation I'm being watched again. For weeks I have had this sensation and it's starting to make me feel like I am losing my fucking mind. Every day on my way to work, at work, and on my way home I feel like this. I grit my teeth, force myself not to think about it, and down my next shot, then chase it down with my gin before signaling the bartender for another round.

I greedily grab the next shot when it's placed in front of me and bring it to my lips, only to pause at the sound of his voice behind me. "Keep drinking like that and you won't know who you're taking home tonight, Miss Noelle."

I close my eyes and fight my body's reaction to his nearness. Being sober and around my boss is fucking hard, but feeling buzzed and having him this close is fucking dangerous. I down the shot and quickly chase it with the next in the hopes it will calm my nerves. I slam the empty shot glass down, then swivel around to face him, only to gasp at how close he is.

I try to fight against the urge to run my gaze over him but I lose the battle. He's wearing a cherry-red pinstripe suit, his black hair slicked back against his head. His blue eyes bore into me, sending a shiver down my spine and making my pussy pulse. The five o'clock shadow that dusts his face only adds to the sexual allure. Nick Snow is a force to be reckoned with and a shark in the boardroom any day of the week, but looking at him right now... I see nothing but my wet dream.

I swallow audibly and take a sip of my gin to gather the courage to even speak to him, but the moment I open my mouth he forces his way between my legs, causing my breath to hitch and my breathing to turn ragged. He reaches out and places his hands on either side of me, caging me in. When he leans down and his breath fans across my face I have to bite back a moan. "Tis the season for giving, Miss Noelle, and you, my little madam, have been giving me signals for months now."

"I have?" I squawk out.

The sexy grin that tugs at the corner of his mouth makes me tremble. That one look has me weak in the fucking knees and my pussy pulsing with the need to be filled and fucked like a cheap slut.

A growl slips out of him, causing my eyes to widen. "You might just be one of the best gifts I have gotten for Christmas." Before I can respond, he pulls back, straightens his suit jacket, pivots on his heel and stalks off. I sit here utterly perplexed and reeling over the encounter we just had. A part of me feels like it was just a dream, a figment of my imagination finally giving me what I have been craving for months, but the lingering scent of his cologne tells me it was real.

"Another round, Miss?" the bartender asks, pulling me from my thoughts. I slowly turn back to face him.

"You just saw my boss, right?" I ask, needing confirmation that I wasn't making this up in my head.

His face scrunches. "You mean Nick Snow?" I nod my head like a fucking idiot. "Yeah, he was definitely here and from what I saw he made himself at home between your legs." My mouth parts and my brows raise while the fucker stands there with a smug smirk on his face. "Don't worry, I'm not judging."

"There isn't anything to judge!" I snap back.

He shrugs. "I'm just the mailroom guy turned bartender for the night. So, can I get you another round?"

I glare at the little fucker. "Yeah. I'm just gonna head to the bathroom, then I'll be back." I don't wait for a response from the little shit. I make my way around the edge of the room, trying to avoid an encounter with someone else. I choose to retreat to the back part of the office where Nick's private bathroom is, the one I use every day when I'm at work. I really don't have a choice since I need to change my tampon and I always leave some in there.

I slip into Nick's office and close the door behind myself, then head for the bathroom. I lock the door and quickly grab a tampon from under the counter before I go about my business.

When I'm done I check my reflection in the mirror and sigh. I look like a buzzed club whore. I take a deep breath and decide for tonight, I don't care. I'm here to drown my sorrows and forget all about my stupid ex.

When I open the bathroom door I freeze at the sight of three men dressed in red silk robes and matching red LED masks with white beards. The masks are lit up, the X's that cover the part shine a bright red, the sticking across the mouth part on the mask seems ominous thanks to the red lights. My breaths turn ragged and my grip on the door handle tightens to the point of pain.

"Well, well, well, look at what we have here, boys." I swallow at the sound of his gruff voice. I can't tell who is speaking. They are all the same height and appear to have the same build and if I hadn't just peed, I would have so pissed myself right now.

"It looks like we have a snack waiting to be devoured and eaten so fucking good she won't remember her own name." My body coils tight with need and my pussy pulses. The encounter with Nick already had me on edge and I'm blaming it on that, not the fact I am getting turned on at the prospect of three masked men fucking me.

The one in the middle steps forward, cementing his place as the alpha of the trio. "Since it's the season of giving, we will allow you a head start."

"What?" I squeak out.

His deep chuckle has the hairs on the back of my neck rising. "You run. We wait, then chase you."

The guy on the right steps forward to stand shoulder to shoulder with the leader. "When we catch you, we're going to devour every fucking inch of that body and mark you as ours."

"Excuse me?" I hiss.

The last guy steps forward and joins the other two. "We've let you have your freedom, watched from afar and now we're tired of wondering what you taste like. We want to own you, consume you, fill you with our release and you're going to love every fucking second of it."

CHAPTER TWO

CHRIS

Her eyes are wide with terror but lurking beneath I see the desire—she's craving this and is trying to rationalize with herself why this is wrong. She can spend an eternity trying to figure that shit out but she won't get the answer she wants, we won't allow it. For months we have watched her, let her be and tried to curb the urges we felt toward her. Not anymore. Holly Noelle will be our new fuck toy and she will enjoy every fucking second of it.

The instant her eyes dart to the door, I grin behind my mask. She's about to play the game. "Run," I grit out.

A small mewl escapes her as she rushes for the door, grips the handle and tries to yank it open, but it won't budge. "What the fuck?" she snaps as she continues to tug at the thing, hoping it will budge. When Saint begins to laugh, she peers over her shoulder and glares at us. She exhales harshly, then releases her grip on the handle and faces us. "Okay," she forces out and places her hands on her hips with a devious look in her eyes. "One, you're all full of shit because you had no plans to allow me to run. Two, how the fuck do you think this thing is going to go down?"

"The only one going down is you, *snowflake*," I purr.

She scoffs. "You think I'm about to let the three of you fuck my brains out in my boss' office, while he is out there with the rest of the staff?" She doesn't give us a chance to answer. "Look around, dipshits, the room has no walls, it's all windows—" Her retort dies on her tongue when my brother pulls a remote out of his pocket, hits a button, then all the windows turn black. We're able to see out but no one is able to see in, but she doesn't need to know that. "Fuck me..." she mutters in shock.

"That's the plan," Nick growls, drawing her attention to him.

She swallows audibly and casts her gaze over each of us before finally settling on my brother. "So, this isn't happening. I have my period and blood and sex just isn't a great mix—"

"Says who?" Saint claps back.

Her face scrunches. "Uh, society?"

"You asking or telling us, snowflake?" I fire back.

She stands there looking stunned for a second

before she wipes the stupor from her face. "You don't care that I have my period?"

Tired of this back and forth, I move toward her, taking slow measured steps so she can feel the tension rising slowly. I'm a masochist, love to torture myself with the prospect of sex and love to drag it out. Judging from the way her body slowly begins to tremble and her breathing turns shallow, she's into it as well. I don't stop until her front is flush against my own. I reach out and grip the back of her neck, forcing her head back to hold my masked gaze.

I use my free hand to trail the tips of my fingers down the front of her sequined dress that has been driving me crazy since the moment she stepped off that elevator. Unable to stop myself, I cup her tit in my palm, relishing in the half gasp half moan that slips out of her. When I pinch her nipple between my fingers, she cries out and pushes onto her tiptoes.

I release her and continue my downward trail until I reach the hem of her dress and push it up to her hips. I peek down to see she is wearing a red lace thong that has me biting the inside of my cheek to keep me from groaning. I cup her pussy and growl my approval at the feeling of her heat in the palm of my hand. Her body tenses for a split second before she relaxes and moans.

I release my hold on her neck, reach into the pocket of my robe and retrieve the blindfold. She eyes it for a second, then darts her gaze back to me.

"Now, before you go overthinking this, don't. I'm

about to take away one of your senses to heighten your others and force you to feel things you never knew you could." I don't wait for her approval, I secure the black silk around her head and steal her vision from her. I look back over my shoulder and nod to Nick and Saint. They make their way toward us and I know the second she can feel their nearness because she begins to tremble.

"Hands behind your back," Nick snaps. She does as he asks. He keeps them in place with his own hand as Saint pushes his mask up to the top of his head, then grips her chin, forcing her to face him. Her mouth parts, but she isn't given a chance to speak as Saint smashes his lips to hers. I relish the sight of my boyfriend feasting on her. I've dreamt about this for months, and finally seeing it happen has me hard as fucking rock.

I drop to my knees before her and push my own mask to the top of my head. Leaning forward, I brush my nose against her pussy and inhale. Her strangled gasp fills the room, making me smirk against her panties.

"I-I... I have my period," she stutters as she breaks the kiss with Saint. She's trying to sound unaffected but we can hear the need in her voice, she fucking wants this.

"Your point?" Nick retorts.

I ignore them as I push her panties to the side and smile at the sight of the string of her tampon. I clamp my teeth down on it and draw back, pulling it out of her pretty little cunt. The instant it's free, she jerks in the guys' hold and fights against Nick to free her arms, but he doesn't budge an inch.

I toss the bloody tampon to the side and ignore her pathetic pleas as I swipe my tongue through her slick folds. Her pleas mute and turn to moans of pleasure as I push my tongue inside her tight, wet pussy. When the metallic taste of her blood hits my tongue, a feral urge overcomes me. I grip her hips and pull her in closer so I can eat the fuck out of her cunt, until she comes all over my face.

"Oh fuck!" she cries out when I suck her clit into my mouth. I insert two fingers inside her and relish in the scream that rips free from her lips. Saint grips her and lifts her ass, giving me better access. I don't waste a second. I increase my tempo and curl my fingers, stroking that sweet spot inside her.

"Take everything he fucking gives you like a good little slut," Nick snarls.

"Yes, give it to me!" she pants out. Her acceptance and eagerness only fuels the desire inside me. I flick my gaze up to watch as Saint pulls the front of her dress down, exposing her creamy tits—her nipples are rock hard and begging to be sucked. Saint looks down at me and grins cockily.

"Take my cock out. You're gonna stroke me while you make her come."

CHAPTER THREE

HOLLY

A strangled moan tumbles out of me at his words as my body heats with need and I wish more than anything that I could watch as he eats my cunt and strokes the other guy's cock. When one of them wraps his hot mouth around my nipple, I scream so loud I fear the rest of the guests will hear me.

Worse, imagine if my fucking boss heard me getting eaten out in his office!

My orgasm is cresting and I start to panic, I'm a squirter and mix that with me having my period it's going to make a fucking mess of this office. My train of thought is cut off when the guy holding my hands bites down on the tender flesh between my neck and shoulder. The bite of pain, mixed with the pleasure the other two are inflicting on me, sends me hurtling over the edge.

"Fuck!" I cry out as my orgasm rips through me like

a cyclone hell bent on destroying a city. Waves of pleasure roll through me. I try to hold back and not squirt, but the second he yanks his fingers out of me and sucks on my clit, I'm fucking done for.

I come all over the guy's face and soak him in my release. Shame washes over me. Chester hated when I made myself squirt and made a mess in his bed. He could never make me come so I was forced to get myself off.

I try to pull my leg free but he won't let go. I struggle in their hold until I feel the gruff stubble of the guy behind me scrape against my cheek.

"Your fight just makes us want this more, snowflake," he says in a gruff tone that's laced with need.

I almost whimper when the guy releases my clit. I sag into the other two, grateful for the reprieve as aftershocks continue to roll through me.

"Get on your fucking knees," the one holding my leg says. I hesitate for a second. They clearly don't like to wait because hands grip my shoulders and force me to the ground. I lift my arms ready to tear the blindfold off but his words have me halting.

"Remove that and this stops. The illusion of being fucked by strangers is what's heightening your need. Give in to your desires and allow us to fulfil them."

My eyes widen behind my blindfold. "How the fuck do you know that?" I hiss.

"Your search history, snowflake." I suck in a sharp

breath. These guys weren't lying about watching me for months. If they have had the time to scroll through my browser history, then they know what I have been searching up in my free time and none of it is PG. I'll admit, being chased and hunted by three masked men and being fucked by strangers has been on the top of my bucket list, but I had never planned on making this wish a reality until... now.

I inhale a deep breath and force all rational thought away. If this is the one chance I have to live out one of my deepest wants, then I am gonna grip this bitch by the fucking horns and ride the damn wave.

I channel my inner bad bitch and let that mother-fucker out to play.

"I want to taste all of you," I purr.

Their answering groans have me smirking. I open my mouth to speak but I'm muted when a cock is thrust into my mouth, making me choke. I try to pull back but then his hand tangles in my hair, keeping me in place.

"Lift your arms and stroke their cocks while I fuck your face, snowflake. Kiss me, baby. I want to taste her cunt off your tongue." I relax my gag reflex and do as he says, picturing the two of them kissing and tasting my cum off the guys tongue. Blindly reaching for the other two, when I grip them both in my hands I moan. They are fucking huge and the girth on them both is fucking thick. These three are going to split me in half and I am fucking here for it! "Fuck, snowflake, you suck me so good, baby."

I moan around him, loving the praise. When he loosens his hold on my hair, I pull back and turn to my left, sucking the other guy. I keep alternating between them, sucking one while stroking the other two. Spit glides down my chin and naked chest, but I don't care. The taste of the three of them is driving me fucking insane with need. I can feel my juices coating the inside of my thighs and forget all about being on my period.

"She sucks our cocks like a good little slut, doesn't she?" one of them says, making me preen from their praise. I hollow my cheeks and suck him deeper as I tighten my hold on the other two, stroking them harder and loving the sounds that escape them. I feel like a goddess. I may be on my fucking knees, but I am the one who holds the fucking power here and it's euphoric.

"Enough!" the guy with his cock in my mouth says and pulls back. I release the other two as I suck in deep breaths. I don't even get a second to gather myself before my arms are grabbed and I'm hauled to my feet. I'm dragged across the room blindly, then cringe when I hear a lot of things crash to the ground.

"Stop!" I snap. "Don't fucking mess this office up or my boss is going to kill me!" I scold.

"The only thing getting murdered tonight, snowflake, is that pussy. This is your only warning. You do not have the upper hand here. You do as we fucking say when we say it. You are not in control." I shiver at the dominance in his tone and love the fact they are stripping me of all control and forcing my inner bad bitch to take a step back.

I squeal when I'm lifted by my hips, and flinch when the cold wood of the desk bites into my bare ass cheeks. I'm pushed backward until my neck hangs over the edge of the desk. I open my mouth to protest, but the words die on my tongue when a cock is thrust inside my mouth. My ankles are lifted to balance on the edge of the desk far enough apart to expose me like a portrait to them.

"Fuck, look at that bloody pussy weeping for us, baby," one of the guys says.

"Eat her pussy while I fuck your ass, baby, then we're going to teach this dirty bitch what *Figging* is." I choke on the cock in my mouth and to my surprise, he pulls out of my mouth, allowing me a chance to breathe.

"Picture my brother fucking my best friend while he eats your cunt and you suck my cock." I whimper but it quickly turns to a moan when I feel a tongue slide through my slick folds. "The sight of your blood all over his face is one of the hottest things I have seen."

"I want to taste it," I blurt, then fight not to cringe. I expect my outburst to ruin the moment, but when I feel the guy between my legs slide up my front, I start to pant.

"Open," he snaps. I do as he says, expecting to feel his tongue slide inside my mouth but instead, he spits into my mouth. I'm in shock but it's quickly replaced by unbridled need when he smashes his mouth to mine. I cannot only taste myself, but I can feel my own blood rubbing off his face onto my own and there is something sick and taboo about this that I fucking want more. I want them to do such depraved sinister things to me.

Forgive me, Santa, I'm about to have your three lookalikes empty their sacks inside me.

Watching Saint smear the blood over her face and force her to taste herself off his tongue has me fisting my own cock. He may be my brother's boyfriend, but we like to share. Saint pulls back when Chris lifts his robe. I smirk when I watch my brother grip the globes of his ass and parts his cheeks, then spits. He lathers his asshole, then spits in the palm of his hand and strokes his cock. Saint buries his face back in her pussy, making her scream. I shove my cock in her mouth to mute her cries.

Chris is a sadistic fuck and doesn't give Saint any warning when he thrusts inside him, making him groan. My brother reaches forward and grips Saint's shoulder so he can fuck him hard and deep. Driven by pure need, I fuck Holly's face like a starved savage, forcing her to take everything I fucking give her.

I match my tempo with my brother's so they both

feel the full force. Holly is already trembling and on the edge of orgasming but the bitch is fighting against it, refusing to give into her body's need. The sound of Saint and Chris's moans mingle with hers, and the sight of them fucking has my cock twitching in her mouth. I reach down and pinch her nipples between my fingers. Her back arches off the table and she moans around my cock. The vibration has me shivering and fighting back my own impending release.

"Let go, you stubborn bitch!" I hiss. My words seem to be her undoing. Her body locks up for a second before she screams around my girth. I pull free of her wet mouth before I lose control and bust a nut. Her screams ricochet off the walls of the office. Chris is groaning and fucking Saint hard, not allowing him to stop eating her cunt. She tries to close her legs but Saint rests his forearms on her thighs, forcing them to remain open.

She tries to push his head away. "I can't... please!" she screams

"Shut the fuck up, you dirty slut," I snap. She shakes her head side to side. She's in a frenzy, her body fighting against her mind. One thinks that she can't come again, while the other is pleading for Saint not to stop. She tangles her fingers in his hair and can't decide if she wants to pull him closer or push him away. Chris tears out of Saint with a pissed off growl. I smirk at my twin. The fucker wants so badly to come, but refuses to miss out on the chance of coming inside her rather than his boyfriend's ass.

"Oh, shit!" Holly screams as her body bows off the desk. A primal scream rents the air as she comes so fucking hard her entire body flushes red. I watch intently as Saint draws back as she squirts all over his face and chest, the silk of his robe turning a dark shade of mahogany from her release. Her cum perfumes the air and draws a long growl of approval from me. When Saint steps back and removes his forearms, her legs drop over the edge and she sinks onto the desk.

I can tell she thinks this is over but she is so fucking wrong.

I move around the desk and grip her waist, pulling her to her feet. She places her hands flat on my chest to try and keep her balance, but it's futile. I spin her around so she is bent over the desk. Like a good little whore she places her palms flat against the wood and turns her head so her flushed cheek is resting against the cool desk. I glide my hands over her plump ass cheeks and relish in the shivers that roll through her. I slowly peel her panties down her legs and then stuff them in my pocket so I can smell her later when I'm at home.

I part her cheeks and kneel down behind her. I spy Chris out of the corner of my eye, on his knees with Saint's cock down his throat. The latter's gaze is fixed on me as I lean forward and swipe my tongue over her puckered hole. She squeals in surprise but she doesn't pull away. As a reward I slap her ass, loving her shriek of surprise.

"My boyfriend's brother is eating your ass while his twin is on his knees, sucking my cock, snowflake," Saint grits out, his voice laced with an edge of need. I push my tongue through her tight muscle wall, relishing the sound of her cry of surprise. "Have you ever had that ass fucked?"

I continue to tongue fuck her ass as she answers, "N-no."

The three of us all groan at her admission. "That shit changes tonight. Your ass is ours and we're going to make sure this is a night for you to remember, baby." She answers Saint with a moan. I reach into my robe pocket and pull out the tube of lube and the small canister of crushed chili.

Holly Noelle is about to get an education in *Figging*.

I pull back and pop the top on the lube and squeeze a generous amount on her hole, then swirl it around and push a finger inside her, stretching her out. She tenses at the intrusion and tries to push up onto her tiptoes to escape me.

"Get your cock out of his mouth and hold her down," I bark. Chris and Saint both groan in annoyance but do as I say. When they stand in front of her, Saint pushes her up forcing me to fall back onto my haunches. He removes his robe and stands there rock fucking hard and proud. He climbs onto the desk and lays flat on his back.

"Climb on, snowflake," he instructs. I roll my eyes and climb to my feet, helping her onto the desk. Saint grips her waist and guides her on top of him. Before he can slip his eager cock inside her cunt, I push her flat against him, stopping their movement and shoot the bastard a wink, which just makes him laugh.

Not wanting to draw this out any longer, I grab the canister of chili and motion for Chris to get the fuck over and hold her cheeks open for me, which he does. I dip my finger into the chili and make sure to coat it nice and good before pulling it out. Chris chuckles and shakes his head, but I know for a fact that my twin loves it when Saint does this to him.

I don't give her any warning when I push my spice-covered finger inside her ass. She lurches forward, but Saint wraps his arms around her and holds her in place.

"It burns!" she cries out.

"It's supposed to. Now shut the fuck up and enjoy the burn before I fill this ass with my cock and make you come on my best friend's dick." She inhales sharply and relaxes slightly. It may burn now, but when you mix that burn with pleasure, it heightens everything. She is going to be begging to try *Figging* again after this encounter. I pull my finger free of her ass, disrobe, then grip my cock in my hand and pump it twice.

Saint takes that as his cue to make his move. He lifts her and shuffles down the desk so I have better access to her ass while he destroys that pussy with his monster cock. She gasps when she feels his head prod at her entrance.

"We're about to make all your Christmas wishes come true, snowflake," Chris promises as Saint thrusts inside her. She throws her head back and screams so fucking loud, I cringe and worry someone from the party may have heard her.

CHAPTER FIVE

HOLLY

I'm burning up and this time not from whatever the fuck is in my ass!

My pussy is stretched out so wide I fear he will tear me in half! I don't get a second to adjust before the guy behind me is parting my cheeks and prodding my tight muscle wall with his dick. I try to relax and take deep breaths, trying to breathe through my anxiety, but it's fucking futile.

"Do you have any idea how long we have dreamed of this moment?" the guy not touching me says.

I shake my head. "No," I pant out as the man behind me pushes forward, drawing a whimper from me. It fucking burns worse than I could have imagined, having a dick in my ass!

"Oh, snowflake. We've been watching you for months. We've seen how unsatisfied you were every time that little cunt would fuck you and leave you to get yourself off." My jaw unhinges at the realization that these three have been stalking me!

Before I can protest, the masked man behind me slams forward and buries himself inside my ass. A blood curdling scream tears out of me, tears prick my eyes and soak through the material of the blindfold. The burning sensation is intensified. It feels like lava is burning me from the inside out. My scream is cut off when a hand clamps down over my mouth. I breathe through my nose trying to block the pain from my mind.

"Distract the bitch!" the guy behind me snaps. The one beneath me begins to move and my breath hitches, it's like a switch has been flicked and the pain is being muted by the need he is stirring inside me.

"Fuck," I pant as I place my hands on his chest and meet him thrust for thrust, making sure to grind down against him. The one in my ass remains still, allowing me to set the rhythm. When I finally find it, I grow confident and push back against him. The groan that slips out of them both emboldens my confidence. Moans tumble out of me and the burn from earlier stops stinging and turns into a pleasure I never knew I could feel.

"Since you can't see anything, I am going to tell you what's happening." I moan in response when the man behind reaches around and cups my tits in his large hands. "I'm about to put my cock in my boyfriend's mouth and let him suck me so fucking good that I come, but he won't be swallowing it. He's going to spit my release into your mouth and you will swallow every last fucking drop. Am I clear?"

I shiver in anticipation. "Yes. I want to taste you," I pant as I slam down onto their cocks and cry out.

"Fuck, she's so tight and the chili is only adding to my fucking pleasure," he says from behind me. His approval only boosts my confidence further and I start to push down onto them harder. The sound of the one beneath me choking on the other guy's dick has me wishing I could watch them.

They aren't wrong, the loss of my sight has forced me to rely on my hearing and feeling. It's like everything feels so much... better.

"That cunt looks so good taking my boy's dick, snowflake," the one in front of me praises.

"He fills me so good," I breathe out as I lean back against the guy behind me. He releases one of my tits and grips my chin, forcing my head back before he claims my lips in a kiss that robs me of air. I melt into him and relinquish control to them fully and trust them to give me what I *need*.

He fucks my mouth with his tongue, in sync with his thrusts. I feel my body coiling with the need to come and I try to stave it off, but I just know they won't allow that to happen. They want to own every one of my releases and I'm at their mercy. I can't do anything except take what they give me and *I fucking love it*.

"Fuck, baby. I'm coming!" I break the kiss and turn

forward, then curse the fucking blindfold for obscuring my view. When he roars it's like a domino effect. I can no longer fight off my own release. It rips through me like an avalanche, my cries of pleasure mingling with his. The aftershocks haven't even finished rolling through when my throat is gripped and I'm pulled forward.

I open my mouth, knowing what's about to happen. When the warm, tangy taste of his cum is spit into my mouth, I swallow it down greedily like a wanton slut needing her fill. Once I have swallowed every drop I feel his tongue lick my lips clean.

"Hmmm, he tastes so good on you, snowflake," he preens as he pulls back and grips my throat in his hand.

All I can muster is a small mewl. I'm utterly spent and my body is begging for a reprieve. I've orgasmed more in this small amount of time than I have in my whole life, and I may actually cry if I come again.

"We're not done yet. Now be a good little bitch and take what the fuck we give you," the one behind me growls. I want to weep and protest but I just know my pleas will fall on deaf ears. When he pulls back I instinctively grind down against the other guy. The heady groan that comes from him has need unfurling inside me. Just when I thought I couldn't take any more, I surprise myself and find that I'm not done after all.

"Oh, God!" I cry out when they both slam inside me at the same time—I feel so fucking full. Their pace is fast and ruthless. I'm nothing but a passenger on this ride as they fuck me hard and raw on this race to them finding their release. My nails dig into his chest as I try to cling onto something to keep me upright.

"Fuck, yes. Take it, you dirty little whore," he pants beneath me.

"Give it to me," I snarl with such conviction it even surprises me.

"I'm gonna come," he shouts from behind me. I prepare myself for his release and accept the fact that I won't be coming with them, but I'm rendered speechless when the man beneath me presses the pad of his thumb against my clit.

"Get there, snowflake." His tone holds a harsh edge to it. I grind against him, chasing my own release but it feels just out of reach, until the one behind me sinks his teeth into the side of my neck, making me scream. The orgasm erupts out of me. Over the sounds of my own cries I hear the both of them roaring out their release and shudder when I feel their cum filling me up. I'm so spent and exhausted I flop forward onto the guy beneath me and close my eyes, needing a moment to just rest.

When I'm slightly lifted so they can pull out of me, I don't protest—.

The thought is halted when I feel two fingers push inside my pussy. I whimper. I can't take it anymore! When he pulls his fingers out of me, I nearly cry with gratitude until he begins drawing something on my back with my blood.

"I thought a candy cane would be a fitting image," I hear him smugly say a second before I surrender to the darkness and allow oblivion to claim me as its sweet sinful prisoner.

CHAPTER SIX

SAINT

I peer down to see she has passed the fuck out, she isn't moving when I poke her side. I snap my gaze to Nick and quirk a brow in question.

"The fuck do we do now?" I ask sarcastically. The plan was to fuck her, have her begging for more and then leave, but now that plan has turned to shit because we fucked her into a coma!

"Put her on the sofa," Nick says.

"She's covered in fucking blood. So are we!" Chris bites back.

When Nick looks at each of us, he sighs and runs a hand through his hair. "Put her on the sofa. We'll clean up while she's passed out, then wake her." Chris gently lifts her off me and carries her to the sofa in the back of the office. He lays her down, then covers her with a throw blanket.

The three of us clean up in the bathroom as best

we can before dressing and placing our masks back on. Once we are done, we move back into the office to find Holly sitting up with a worried look on her face. She looks at each of us, then nibbles on her bottom lip.

"What now?" she whispers. I bite back my smirk.

"When we call, you answer. Deny us and you won't like what happens." Her eyes widen but she says nothing in response to Nick's statement. Without uttering another word, the three of us leave the room.

We don't head back to the party, we take the elevator in the back that is reserved for Nick and head down to the parking garage. Once we all pile into my car, I peel out of there. Only when we are a block away do we remove our masks.

"I'm keeping her," I announce. Chris chuckles beside me, then reaches over and places his hand on my thigh and squeezes.

"She's ours now, baby. One taste will never be enough where she is concerned," he says.

Nick snorts in the backseat. "She's cleaning my office." Chris and I both chuckle. Holly is a clean freak and the mess we made in that office would have hit a nerve. Her apartment is spotless, everything has a place and every place has a thing—our girl has a bit of OCD.

My phone rings through the Bluetooth system in the car, and without checking the caller ID I hit answer. "Yeah?"

"Saint, where the fuck is she?" I grip the steering

wheel tighter and grind my teeth. Chris and Nick both snarl in hatred at the sound of my little brother's voice.

"No idea who you are talking about," I say evenly.

The little shit scoffs. "She works at your fucking company. I know she had a party there tonight and now she isn't answering my calls." I roll my lips over my teeth to keep from smiling.

"Why on earth would your *girlfriend*," I drag the word out just to be a prick, "not be answering your calls?" My boys both shake with silent laughter.

"Look, asshole, I was attacked in my apartment earlier today by three masked pussies."

"Oh, no, are you hurt?" I ask in a mocking tone.

"Fuck you, Saint!" he roars. "They used my fucking phone and broke up with her and now she won't answer my calls and let me explain." I have to bite the inside of my cheek to keep from laughing. "The holidays are coming up and she was supposed to come with me to the cabin to meet Mom and Dad!"

"Oh boo-fucking-hoo, you little shit!" I snap. "You never deserved her anyway. She's better off without you. Stop pouting like a little bitch and fuck off." I end the call without remorse. My brother and I don't get along at all. He hates that I have a boyfriend and can't get over that I like to suck dick. The truth is, he just uses that as an excuse. He fucking hates that I don't need to live off Mom and Dad, and the companies that I started never failed, they thrived. He's always been a jealous little shit and I've never wanted anything he's had, until *her*.

"Dumb bitch's mouth is writing a check his ass can't cash." I force a laugh for Chris's benefit, I know he is trying to keep from spiraling but, it's too late. My brother may be welcome at my parents' cabin, but I just get the pity invite because they feel they have to have me there. Doesn't look good when the infamous North's own son doesn't come home for the holidays.

The weekend passes by without a hitch. I've never been more excited for it to be a fucking Monday!

Chris and I don't work on the same floor as Nick and Holly, but as of today, Holly is about to not only answer to Nick but to us as well. We have staff working round the clock over the weekend to make the preparations needed to accommodate the expansion on Nick's office.

"Let's go, I want to get there before she does," Nick calls out as he heads for the front door. Chris rubs his hands together, then shoots me a wink.

"Let's go introduce ourselves to the snowflake." I smirk at my boy and slap his ass as he walks past.

The drive to the office takes half the time. I broke the speed limit the entire way and feel no fucking guilt over it. We head up to the twenty-eighth floor, it's empty except for Sharon, the front receptionist, who greets the three of us with a smile, then hands us each our mail, Post-it notes with reminders and then lets us know our office is ready. Nick leads the way. As we stalk down the hallway, memories of what we did Friday night assault me and I'm instantly fucking hard.

The ghost of her screams echo around me as we enter the revamped office. The three of us stand shoulder to shoulder in the entrance and take in the sight. All three of our desks are against the windows, Holly's desk against the far wall directly in front of us, giving us a clear view of her *all* day long.

"Keep your fucking cool, he may be your brother but it won't stop him and your father from trying to sink us. We need this deal, and him losing his girlfriend should keep him distracted long enough for us to finish this merger." If anyone else aside from Nick said that shit to me I would have broken their nose. Not him though. I know he is only saying this because he cares and only wants to see me prosper.

"Come on, let's get ready for the snowflake to arrive," Chris says as he claps us both on the shoulder and heads for his desk.

I look over at Nick and grin. "Today is going to be the best fucking day."

His brows furrow. "Why?"

"Because I get to sit next to you and watch you squirm all fucking day long, knowing you can't touch her or you'll blow our little plan."

His eyes darken. "You're the one sporting a hard on."

I shrug. "Difference is, I can have your brother's lips around my cock anytime I want."

A sinister look flashes across his face. I grunt when he grips the front of my shirt and yanks me flush against him. "Careful, baby, you know my brother gets off on watching you suck my cock."

Motherfucker's got me there!

"Now that you mention it, we have an hour before she gets here and I for one am down to watch my boyfriend give you head while I watch and stroke one out," Chris grits out. I glance over at him out of the corner of my eye to see him standing behind his desk and already unbuttoning his pants.

"Fuck it," I mutter as I drop to my knees.

"Good fucking choice," Nick praises as I begin to unfasten his belt. "Suck my cock like a good slut and I might just let my twin fuck you before she gets here."

CHAPTER SEVEN

HOLLY

The events of Friday night have been playing on a loop non-stop in my head over the weekend. I'm fucking terrified to head into the office and see my boss. Would he know? Did I clean up enough? One of the glass paperweights on Nick's desk was destroyed when one of the guys swiped everything off it. I don't know if it held any meaning to him or not and if he notices it missing... what the fuck am I going to say?

I'm so sorry, Mr. Snow. It was broken during my sexcapade with masked men who fucked me like a cheap whore on your desk.

The ride up to the office in the elevator is agony. I'm dreading the doors opening and seeing my stuff in a box on the top of the reception desk, signaling that I'm fired and he knows what I did. When the doors open, I nearly drop to my knees in gratitude when I don't see a box on Sharon's desk. I tentatively step out, only to pause a second later when my phone begins to vibrate in my hand.

I look down and grit my teeth at the sight of Chester's name. I hit ignore. Who the fuck calls the person they broke up with nonstop and constantly texts them? My stupid ass ex, that's who. I wave hello to Sharon and a few others as I make my way to the back toward Nick's office. My palms are clammy and my breathing is choppy. I keep my head down the entire way and when I step into his office, I jerk my head up at the sound of voices.

My eyes widen at the sight before me. The office is... revamped. Everything has changed. Not only has my desk been moved, but two others are now in here and they are occupied by... wait. One of the guys looks exactly like my boss except I can see tattoos covering his neck and hands. I look at the guy seated in the middle desk who has his phone pressed to his ear and his gaze focused on the screen in front of him. He looks nothing like Nick and I sigh with gratitude, but he is fucking hot as sin.

"Miss Noelle." I snap my head to the right and lock eyes with my boss. Jesus, I need to get myself under control. Friday night was one for the books, but the memory of Nick making himself at home between my legs burns like a still shot in my mind's eye. Nick Snow is sinfully beautiful—he's a bad boy wrapped in an Armani suit.

"Y-yes, Sir?" I clear my throat and try not to cringe

at the high-pitched sound of my voice. He rises to his feet and buttons his suit jacket before rounding his large desk, the very same desk I came on more times than I care to count. Nick doesn't stop until he is standing directly in front of me, forcing me to crane my neck back in order to maintain eye contact with him.

"As you can see I've made some changes." I nod like an idiot. "Allow me to introduce you to your new bosses."

My brows hit my hairline. "Are you leaving?" I shout, then cringe and smile sheepishly up at him.

He shakes his head. "No," is all he says, then turns on his side to allow me to see the other two men who are now staring right at me. He points to the guy who was just on the phone. "Saint North, meet Holly." Saint grins wickedly and those fucking dimples have me weak in the knees and the intense look in his green eyes has me biting the inside of my cheek. I can already tell Saint is trouble and if I don't watch myself, it won't just be my boss I am envisioning fucking each day. Nick points to the guy on the end who is a spitting image of himself. "Chris, meet Holly."

Chris smiles wide and winks. I fight not to groan, the man is fucking lethal just to look at. My panties won't last the day at this rate. "Nice to meet you, darlin'," he drawls.

"Uh, you same too," I screech. "I mean, same to you!" I feel my shame coat my cheeks and wish the ground would open up and swallow me fucking whole!

The three of them laugh at my expense which only serves to heighten my shame, so I drop my gaze to the floor.

Nick grips my chin and forces my head up to meet his burning gaze. The dominant look in his blue eyes has my pussy quivering and knees weak. "It appears my twin has you all tongue tied." His tone has an edge and is almost suggestive but I refuse to let my mind wander down that track.

I peer over at Chris from the corner of my eye to find him grinning at us. I fucking knew they were too similar in looks not to be related. I clear my throat and manage to gather myself before stepping out of Nick's grasp and forcing a small smile to my face.

"Lovely to meet you both, if you need anything, let me know." I head to my desk and do my damndest not to look over at the three of them. I thought working alone with Nick was bad, but having all three of these gods in the same confined space with me daily is going to be fucking torture.

For three days I have been working until close to ten at night. Nick, Saint and Chris have stayed behind with me. I've been attending meetings with them and taking notes, and scouring over the paperwork for this merger they have coming up. From what I can tell, this merger is the biggest deal they will ever make in their careers and it's really weighing on them.

Nick and I get along great, he's been nothing but good to me since he hired me and I worried that our dynamic would change when Saint and Chris joined us, but I was wrong. The two of them are amazing. I hate to admit it but I was fucking bummed when I found out they were dating each other. My dreams of having my very own harem were obliterated, but it hasn't stopped me going home every night and rubbing my clit to dreams of the three of them fucking me.

I would give anything for my masked men to come back and take another turn on me just to relieve me of this ache. No matter how many times I make myself come, I'm just never satisfied.

"Holly?" I look up from my computer.

"Yeah, Saint?"

I fucking swoon when he smiles, the guy is fucking heroin to my pussy, the dirty bitch is wet twenty-four-seven. "We have to head out now. When you get done with those charts, head home." I nod my head and smile my thanks.

"There will be a car waiting for you to take you home." I shake my head but Chris raises a hand, silencing my argument. "No walking for you tonight. Head down to the garage and our driver will be waiting." The three of them stalk out of the office without allowing me to say another word. The bad bitch inside me wants to riot and tell them I can get my own ass home, but then the girly girl inside me swoons at how thoughtful they are.

My pussy pulses with need. I glare down at her and narrow my eyes. "We are not going to fuck our bosses, ever. We're destined for mediocre cock and constantly getting ourselves off until our friends from Friday appear again," I scold.

Santa, if your listening to my prayers, please send me back those masked look-alikes, because ya girl needs to get fucked!

CHAPTER EIGHT

CHRIS

I stand behind the column in the entryway, patiently waiting. My cock has been rock hard for days and no matter how many times I rub one out or fuck Saint, the ache remains. I need to be inside her again. I need to feel her warm mouth wrapped around my cock and hear the sounds of her cries as my brother and Saint fuck her. I want to see her break apart beneath us.

When the front door opens, my breath hitches as excitement rolls through me. None of us move until she closes the door. When I hear the lock click into place, I make my move. Before she can flick the lights on, I hit the switch on my mask to turn the red LED lights on. I rush forward and wrap my arm around her waist and clamp my other hand over her mouth to mute her scream.

She kicks out and throws her arms around, trying

to break free of my hold. The second the other two hit the switch on their masks I spin her around to face them. When she spots them she stops fighting against me and relaxes in my hold. I roll my eyes, this fucking girl is something else. She should be petrified and fighting harder to get away from us. We fucked her like crazed psychos in my brother's office, wore masks and bent her to our will, yet here she is, relaxed and trembling with need in my hold over the fact three masked strangers are inside her home ready to make her dirtiest dreams come true.

"Release her," Nick says in a deep tone. He's trying to mask the sound of his voice. This time around, we chose to forgo the beards since they got in the fucking way last time. I move to stand with the guys, putting Saint in the middle of me and Nick. Our masks offer us enough light to see her. Her mouth is ajar as if she wants to say something but then snaps it closed.

The shocked look on her face morphs into one of pure seduction. She shucks off her coat, letting it drop to the floor. My brows raise behind my mask, surprised at her bold move. When she reaches for the buttons on her blouse, my cock twitches. She keeps her gaze on us as she begins to give us the best striptease I have ever seen. I'm hanging onto every single movement she makes. When she finally pops the last button, she doesn't remove it. She glides a finger down the middle of her chest, teasing us with a moan. She stops at the waist of her pencil skirt that hugs her perfectly.

She reaches behind her and begins to slowly drag the zipper down, making us wish for a fast forward button but at the same time loving how she is torturing us with this foreplay.

"For five days, all I have thought about is the way you three owned me." Her sultry voice only heightens my need for her. When the skirt drops to the ground, she removes her blouse and steps forward. She stands like a fucking goddess, in a white bra and panty set that's matched with stockings and a garter belt, pair that shit with the red heels she wears and we have a wet fucking dream. She reaches up and pulls the elastic from her hair, then shakes her head, allowing the beautiful raven strands to fall around her shoulders and face. "I've spent three days locked in that office with my boss, his brother and their friend." At the mention of us, I feel Saint tense beside me.

"Did you picture how we fucked you and made you come all over his desk?" Saint asks in a gravelly tone.

She closes her eyes and moans, then cups her full tits in her hands, making me bite down on my lip or I risk groaning out loud. "Yes. Every day I think about it. I'm constantly wet."

"Are you wet for them or for us?" I push, my tone is filled with hunger.

She cuts her gaze to me and keeps it there as she trails a hand down her flat stomach and then cups her pussy, making herself gasp. "Both." Her honesty astounds me, but at the same time, fills me with pride knowing she is just as bothered by our presence at work as we are of her. "I picture them fucking me just like you did. Then I picture the three of you and how good it felt when you ate my ass and fucked my pussy only to have the taste of one of you in my mouth. I've been a bad girl," she admits.

"How bad, snowflake?" Nick hedges.

She looks over at him as she pushes her panties to the side and glides a finger through her folds, moaning. I've never been jealous of a fucking finger before but it appears there is a first time for everything. "So bad. I play with my pussy every night and make myself come but it's never enough. I need to feel you inside me, filling me and stretching my greedy cunt out just to accommodate your size. I even get myself off at work when the bosses step out for lunch." My fucking jaw hits the floor, we've all been watching her on the cameras in the office and never once have we seen her do that.

"At your desk?" Saint questions.

"Fuck," she pants when she pushes a finger inside herself.

"Answer!" Nick snaps.

She's too turned on to heed the bite in his tone. She lolls her head forward and has a dazed-out look in her eyes as she looks at him. "No." She widens her legs to give herself better access. "I hide in the bathroom and get myself off."

I can't stop myself, I slide my hand inside my robe and grip my cock. I hiss, drawing her attention to me. She smirks at the sight of me stroking my cock.

"I have a surprise for you," she says in a husky tone. The three of us stand here, watching her as she turns around, giving us her back. I bite my lip at the sight of her bare ass cheeks. She grips the waistband of her thong and slowly bends forward, pulling it down her legs. When it is around her ankles and she is folded in half, she reaches back and grips her cheeks, then parts them.

"Fuck."

"Goddammit."

"Snowflake," the three of us all say in unison at the sight of the glistening diamond stud in her ass.

"After Friday, I haven't been able to stop thinking about how good it felt to have all my holes filled."

"You go to work with that in every day?" Saint grits out as he takes a step forward.

She looks right at him through the gap in her legs. "Every... single... day." She's playing this vixen roll so fucking well, to the point she has the three of us eating out of the palm of her fucking hand right now. She stands and then turns to face us, looking like a goddess. She reaches back and unclasps her bra, then tosses it to the side. She's bare aside from the heels, garter belt and stockings, and now I know this is my new favorite look on her.

"Lights off," Nick barks. The three of us kill the

lights on our masks, then remove our robes so she can see the surprise we have waiting for her. It's time for snowflake to suck our cocks like they are candy canes before we destroy her cunt for anyone else.

CHAPTER NINE

HOLLY

My jaw unhinges and my eyes widen, it's pitch black in here except for... their cocks. I mean that literally!

They are lit up like a fucking Christmas tree.

They have covered their dicks in glow in the dark paint. Needing a closer look, I move toward them, the only sound in the room is my heels clicking against the hardwood floor. I stop a step away and drink in the sight of their artwork. They have decorated themselves in red and white paint to make their cocks look like candy canes!

"Don't worry, snowflake, it's edible paint," the one directly in front of me says. The fact he thinks I would even care if the paint wasn't is cute. I don't wait for their directions, I slowly lower to my knees, loving the feeling of their gazes on me the entire time. It's an empowering feeling knowing these three men are relying on me to give them the release they crave.

I dart my tongue out and lick the underside of one cock, loving the sound of his pained groan. I jerk back in surprise when the flavor bursts on my tongue.

"Flavored paint?" I question.

The guy in front of me chuckles. "Mint and cherry, now wrap those fucking lips around my cock, you teasing bitch." I obey his command and wrap my lips around him, the taste of him mixed with the cherry and mint has me moaning. It's a strange mixture but fucking addictive. When the other two step forward, I grip them and begin stroking. The sounds coming from the three of them fills my apartment and I love it.

I switch between the three of them, stroking and sucking, making sure to pay them all equal attention. I may not know their faces or be able to see their masks, but I can definitely tell them apart by their cocks. They're all huge, not just in length but girth as well. My mouth is aching from being stretched so wide but the reward is going to be worth the pain.

"Fuck yes, snowflake," the one on my right says.

"I want to come on your face," the one in the middle says. I moan my agreement. I want them to cover me in their release and mark me as theirs once again. With their impending release hanging in the distance, I quicken my strokes and bob faster. I switch between them like a well-oiled machine, I can feel they are all close. Before I can finish sucking the one on my left off, he pulls free of my mouth and I pout.

"Stay there." The three of them press in closer so

the tips of their cocks skim my face as they continue to stroke themselves. I open my mouth and poke out my tongue, waiting for them to cover me.

"Fuck," the one on my right roars, then I feel jets of his cum hit the side of my face. The one on my left is the next, followed by the one in the middle. I gasp as their cum hits me and close my eyes. I moan when some of it lands on my tongue and greedily swallow it like it's my favorite treat.

I gasp and snap my eyes open when I feel a hand begin to smear the cum all over my face, coating it like a facemask. I expect him to stop there but then I squint my eyes in the dark and watch as the one in the middle lifts his hand to his face then turns his back to me, my brows furrow in confusion until I hear him moan. My jaw slackens, he just... tasted all of their releases.

"Your turn, baby," one of them says, then I'm being hoisted to my feet by my arm and dragged across the room to the sofa. "On your knees, hands on the back and keep those legs open." I eagerly obey his command and situate myself on the couch like he instructed. I feel the three of them behind me and want to look back over my shoulder, but what's the fucking point? I can't see shit thanks to the blackout shutters I had installed a few months ago.

I jerk forward and cry out when he smacks my ass. It stings but when he begins to rub that spot it takes the bite away. He repeats this four more times. I'm panting and trembling with need. I knew I was into some kinky shit but I didn't realize how much. I tense when I feel him grip the butt plug. He slowly pulls it out of me and the instant it's free, I feel empty.

I hear footsteps and when I feel one of them in front of me, I lift my head. "Open," is all he says in that deep growly tone. I do as I'm told and open my mouth. I balk when I feel the cool metal of the butt plug in my mouth. I attempt to pull back but he tangles his fingers in my hair and holds me in place as he uses the plug to fuck my mouth. "You dirty little slut, you're lucky I'm not punishing you for taking away my joy in being the one sliding this inside your ass for the first time." The slut inside me preens, while the rational side of me screams that it's my body and I can do what the fuck I want with it.

My train of thought is rendered silent when I feel something being pushed inside my ass. I can tell just from the feeling that it isn't a cock or a dildo, the texture is... different. I tense and keep sucking the butt plug so it doesn't continue to hit my teeth.

"Google tells us that you wanted to try *Nyotaimori*." I go still at the mention of *that*. The fucker behind me laughs and continues to push what-ever it is inside me. The one in front removes the butt plug. I begin panting and burning up all over. "Have you ever heard of a giant candy cane, snowflake?" My eyes widen and I tense, only fueling his laughter. "That's right, baby, you have a candy cane in your ass and if you're a good little slut I'll let my boyfriend suck on it."

Yes, I did search up what Nyotaimori was and I was curious about it, but I didn't think I would get to experience it. Now that it's happening, I'm terrified to know what other items they have to use for my two remaining holes!

"Holy shit," I pant and begin shaking, it's so fucking deep and the fact it's sliding inside me with ease just shows how well those plugs have stretched me.

"There," he announces proudly. I almost weep with joy. There is no way I could have taken it any deeper than it is and I can still feel some of it hanging out of me. "Next. Baby, would you like the honors?"

"Yes." I feel them change spots behind me and try my best to remain relaxed and not panic. "Easy snowflake, this one is gonna be as good for you as it will be for me." His words do nothing to put me at ease. I shiver when I feel something plastic with a point prod at my entrance. I try to shift and close my legs, but the one in front of me tugs on the strands of my hair making me yelp.

"Close those fucking legs and I'll chain your ass up and use my belt on that ass." His sinister promise should have me balking, but instead I'm more fucking aroused at the prospect of him spanking me. "Such a filthy slut," he coos, then strokes my cheek with the tips of his fingers. I can't help but look at his cock, it's still glowing and I hunger for another taste—

"Fuck," I cry out in fright when I hear a can spray then feel something being pushed inside me.

"Banana covered in whipped cream for this dirty pussy," the guy says from behind me. My eyes roll back and I flop forward over the back of the sofa when he begins to fuck with me the fruit. "You like that, don't you?"

"Hmmmm," I moan.

A yelp escapes me when my ass is spanked. "Answer my boyfriend, you greedy cunt."

"Yes!" I scream out when he pushes the banana deeper inside me. "It feels so fucking good." I feel full but it's still not enough.

I need to feel *them* inside of me.

My chin is gripped and my head is lifted. "You get to choose, either my cock in your mouth or an item of food of my choosing?" he says. I open my mouth to answer, but the words die on my tongue as a scream tears out of me when I feel a mouth begin sucking on my pussy and another bobbing up and down on the candy in my ass. "Think fast, snowflake, I'm not a patient man."

"Cock!" I scream out when I feel the candy and the banana begin to move inside me from their sucking. "I choose your cock—" The rest of my sentence is cut off when he rams his dick down my throat. The sound of my gagging fills the room. I push back against the other two as I grip his waist and pull him in closer, needing more... I don't know what *more* is but I just need something extra.

I cry around him when the candy cane is slowly pulled from my ass. I feel like I'm on fire. If this is what is feels like to burn in hell, then sign me the fuck up, Lucifer, because I'm coming to spend eternity with you!

When I feel the nozzle of the can push into my tight hole I don't tense. He squirts the cream into my ass and I shiver in anticipation. The moment the nozzle is replaced with his tongue, I fucking lose it. I scream around the dick in my mouth and grind their faces, chasing my release.

"Look at what a good little slut you are," he preens as he thrusts into my mouth. "One night with us and now you're a whore for having your ass eaten out." Hearing him call me a slut only has me coiling with need—this is how I wanted Chester to talk to me when we were fucking, wanting to use me, own me, force me to submit to his will and demand everything of me, but he was too fucking vanilla and only cared about getting himself off.

When the banana is yanked out of me and they both stop eating me out, I want to scream out at the injustice until one of them drops down onto the sofa beside me. The grip he has on my hair vanishes and I release him from my mouth, without being prompted I shift and straddle the guy's lap. I reach between our bodies and guide his cock to my entrance. I lower onto him slowly, savoring the burn of how good he feels, fitting inside me and stretching out my pussy.

Once he is fully sheathed inside my tight cunt, we cry out. I don't get a moment to enjoy the feeling before a hand lands on my back and pushes me forward.

"Hold that ass open for me, baby." The one beneath me reaches around and parts my cheeks. I'm so fucking wet and needy, I've never been this turned on in my life and the feeling is fucking addictive. I moan when I feel the head of his cock slowly press inside me.

"Oh God, yes," I breathe out, this time the burning sensation is from being stretched and not from fucking chili.

"Want to know a secret, snowflake?" the guy under me whispers in my ear, the cool plastic of his mask against my face is like a balm.

"Yes," I pant.

"They're brothers and I sucked both their cocks on the way over here." His crude words have my eyes widening. I thought they were only saying they are brothers to play into some kink but now, I don't think that's the case. "Open your mouth and suck my boyfriend's brother's cock while we fuck you." Utterly strung out with need and unable to form a response, I do as he says.

The feeling of her hot little mouth wrapped around my dick is better than I remember. The girl has fucking skill and it's not learned, it's just a natural fucking talent she has. Chris grunts in pleasure when he's balls deep in her ass, the vibration from her moans sends shivers up my spine. I jerk in surprise when she draws back and strokes me with her hand while sucking on my balls.

"I need you to move!" Saint grits out, he sounds pained and that shit makes me smile. He's the worst cock tease but he can suck dick just as good as she can. Chris and I may share but we have never crossed swords. We've had threesomes with Saint and I fucking love that shit but never before have we had a foursome until Friday night.

The three of them all moan when Chris begins to fuck her, sending her jerking forward. Her grip on my dick tightens to the point of pain, making me hiss. I grip her hair in my hand and yank hard. She cries out in pain.

"You break it, you will fucking regret it." Even in the dark I swear I see the little bitch's eyes narrow in challenge.

"Don't come in my mouth, I want a double cream pie," she pants out as she bounces up and down on the guys, trying to reclaim control. The stupid bitch was never in control, we allowed her the illusion of it but nothing more.

"You get what I fucking give." I bat her hand away and step back, leaving her to fuck my brother and Saint while I watch.

"This ass is mine, snowflake," Chris grunts as he pumps into her.

"Yes," she agrees.

"Bet your bosses don't fuck you like this," I spit out.

"No, but I wish they did." Her response has me stilling. "Fuck, I'm gonna come," she shouts. I flick the light on the mask, needing to see her break apart. Chris grips her legs and lifts her off Saint, holding her up. Saint leans forward and rubs her clit. She throws her head back and screams. When she comes, it's like watching the best porn movie you've ever seen. She is the sexiest woman I have ever laid eyes on. She squirts all over Saint and both guys growl their approval before Chris is placing her back on Saint's lap.

"Fuck me hard," she snaps as she begins bouncing on them again. "I need you to fill me with your cum."

"That what you want, snowflake?" Saint grits out and then groans.

"Yes, I want to feel you inside me," she pleads.

"I'm close, after I come, my brother is going to fuck this ass," Chris promises.

"Please..." she begs.

"Get ready, baby, I'm about to fill this ass," my twin vows.

"Fuck, I won't last," Saint shouts.

"Don't you fucking come!" I snap. Saint groans in displeasure but doesn't respond. The sofa begins screeching along the floor as Chris's thrusts turn punishing. To her credit, she takes everything they are giving without complaint. Her cries are bouncing off the walls and filling me with a sense of pride, knowing we are the ones who are doing this to her. I love the sight of my brother and Saint both inside her, I could watch them take turns on her all fucking day and never tire of the sight. My mouth waters with the need to taste her but I can't risk her seeing me.

Fucking my assistant is a huge breach and if she was to find out why I really hired her, she could sue my ass.

"Fuck!" Chris roars as he comes, not able to wait another second. I dart around the couch and yank him back. The bastard just laughs, but I ignore him as I line up my cock and thrust inside her, making her scream.

"You like that dick in your ass, you dirty cum slut?" I snarl as I grip her waist in a bruising hold and slam into her hard and deep, forcing her to take everything I fucking have to give.

"I can't last," Saint pants.

"Yes the fuck you can," I grit out through clenched teeth.

"Oh shit, I'm coming!" Saint bellows. I growl in annoyance while Holly's screams continue to fill the room.

"Robe on!" I snap at my brother. I'm too pissed off at Saint for coming to care what he has to say. I pull out of her, then grip her waist and lift her off him. She whirls around and faces me but I don't give her a chance to question me. I lift her and then carry her across the room. She wraps her arms and legs around me.

I hit the switch for her blinds and allow the moonlight to bathe the room. We're all wearing our masks and Chris's tattoos will be covered by his robe. Her eyes are wide and filled with wonder. I move until we are in front of the large window that looks over the city. I place her on her feet, then spin her around so she is looking out at all the people below us and the cars.

"What are you doing?" she breathes out.

"Shut the fuck up," I snap back, then kick her legs open. "Hands flat on the glass." She does as I say and bends forward, giving me better access. I push forward and sheath myself inside her tight wet cunt.

"Shit," she cries out. I press my thumb into her ass and begin finger fucking it in sync with my thrusts. "Just like that," she barks as she starts pressing back against me. "Oh fuck, I'm gonna come!" When I feel her pussy begin to clamp down on my cock, I don't stop, I keep fucking her harder, needing to feel her cover my dick in her cum. When her cries of pleasure rent the air, I finally pull out of her and relish the feeling of her cum soaking my front. I give myself a second to enjoy the feeling before I'm slamming back inside her cunt.

I grip her hair in my free hand and use it as leverage so I can push inside her harder. Her breath is fogging the glass but her fear of being seen is long gone now as the pleasure rolls through her. I want every motherfucker to see me fucking her so they know she belongs to us.

She's ours!

I feel my balls tighten and know I am about to erupt and fill this pussy with my cum, but I need her orgasm... I need her to break one more time before I allow myself the pleasure of marking her as mine.

"Give it to me, snowflake," I grit out.

"I can't," she whimpers. Before I can form a response, Saint comes to stand beside us, then reaches under her and circles her clit, making her scream louder. Chris comes to my other side and pinches her nipples, driving her fucking mad with need. "Oh shit."

"Fucking take it, give me what the fuck I want," I roar.

"Motherfucker!" she screams as she detonates. Her legs give out, the only thing keeping her up is our hold on her. I follow her over the edge of oblivion and see fucking stars as I empty everything I have inside her. Shudders roll through me as I ride the high of my release. When she jerks forward I keep her in place.

"I can't... please," she says barely above a whisper. She sounds utterly wrecked and I fucking preen.

"For tonight, we're done, but never forget we're watching you, snowflake, so the next time you want to get yourself off at work, do it behind your desk so we can see."

I'm dead on my feet as I walk into the office the next morning. When one of my masked men carried me to the couch, I passed out. I have no idea how they got into my apartment or managed to lock the door after themselves, but they did.

"Morning, sunshine." I look and force a smile at Saint. He looks bright and chipper while I feel like death on legs.

"Morning," I mutter as I head for my desk.

"Rough night?" Nick asks.

I cringe, then plaster on a fake, cheery smile and shake my head. "Nope. Just went straight home," I answer.

"You look like someone beat that ass." My eyes widen at Chris's remark.

I shake my head vigorously. "No, no beating. Just home and bed." The three of them purse their lips as if they are trying to hide their smiles, which just pisses me off. "Anything pressing this morning that needs to be handled?" I say, trying to redirect the conversation.

"You've handled us well," Saint says. Call me crazy but I feel like there is a double meaning to that comment, which I refuse to dwell on. It's one thing picturing my masked men as my bosses, but it's another thing to be at work and envisioning them railing me and taking turns as they fuck me bare. I drop my gaze to my diary and choose to ignore responding as I delve into my tasks for the day.

I'm on fucking edge!

All day these three have made sure to brush against me or find some reason to touch me and it's driving me crazy! Coming into work everyday and seeing them is hard enough, but them touching me is like adding gas to a simmering fire.

I'm about to combust.

It's too much, yet not enough. Jesus, I need to get my fucking head checked. Last night I had my brains fucked out and still I am thirsting for more. Not from my masked men but from my damn bosses, and that's not fucking cool!

"We're heading out to lunch. Want anything?" I shake my head and wave them off as they leave. The second the door closes behind the three of them, I slouch in my seat and release a pent up sigh. I have half an hour tops before they get back. I move to stand, but then remember his words from last night.

Never forget we're watching you, snowflake, so the next time you want to get yourself off at work, do it behind your desk so we can see.

I nibble on my lip for a second, debating if I should take the risk or not. When my need wins out, I reach for the remote on my desk and click the button to turn the windows dark so no one can see in. I push back from my desk and widen my legs, lifting my skirt to expose my black lace thong.

"If you are really watching me, then this is for you," I say to the empty room. I push my panties to the side and slide a finger through my slick folds and moan—I'm fucking drenched. Unable to tease myself and just needing the euphoria my release will give me, I push two fingers inside my cunt and bite down on my lip to keep from crying out. I use my free hand to cup my tit and pinch my nipple through my blouse, making me arch my back.

I can hear how fucking wet I am and I find no guilt in making a mess of my seat as I finger my pussy hard and deep. I throw my head back and swallow my cry of pleasure as I hit that sweet spot. I use my thumb to press against my clit and have to bite down on my lip to remain silent. My breathing is ragged, a fine sheen of sweat coats my body. My eyes scrunch shut as I picture my masked men removing their masks to reveal their faces. Saint, Nick and Chris stand before me, ready and waiting to fuck me.

"You've been a bad slut." Nick growls in my dream

"Yes." I pant aloud.

"You want our cocks?" Saint asks.

"I've been a bad slut," I respond to the voice in my head.

"Get on your knees and suck our cocks," Chris snaps.

"Yes, give me your cocks. I want the three of you to fill me up," I pant out a second before I detonate all over my fingers. A silent scream tears out of me. I yank my fingers free, not wanting to squirt all over the office floor and slouch back against my chair. The orgasm took the edge off but it did little to satisfy the hunger burning in the pit of my gut.

"I'd rather eat her than this." I jerk upright at the sound of Saint's voice. My eyes are bugging out of my head at the sight of all three of them standing there looking right at me. I jump to my feet and pull my skirt down to try and save some of my fucking dignity. How did I not hear the fucking door open or close? Oh, that's right, you were talking to yourself, you dumbass!

The four of us stand here for a long time not uttering a word, shame coloring my cheeks. I'm trying to think of a lie to explain why my pussy was just out, but no amount of bullshit is going to fool them into thinking I wasn't just fingering myself.

"I can explain," I blurt. Chris quirks a brow as he pops a chip into his mouth. It's only then that I notice they are carrying snacks in their hands... They went to the vending machine down the hall.

Fuck!

The one fucking time they don't go out to eat, I decide to get risky and get fucking caught!

Nick is fighting back a smile as he leans his shoulder against the wall. "Oh, I can't wait to hear this," he says, making me cringe. Saint doesn't even try to hide his smile. Chris on the other hand just looks like the fucking cat that got the canary.

They are loving this.

"I was... umm... I was—"

"Flicking the bean?" Chris supplies earning a glare from me.

"Playing with yourself?" Saint adds, which just has me scrunching my face.

"No?" It comes out like a question and I hate myself for that.

"So, we didn't just walk in on you orgasming on your fingers?" Nick asks. The humor in his tone isn't lost on me.

I throw my hands in the air in frustration. "Yeah, okay. You totally busted me finger fucking myself. Happy now?" I bite out.

"Oh, I'm ecstatic," Nick volleys back.

"Best thing I've seen," Saint tacks on.

"I agree with Saint, you look more tasty than this shit." I balk at Chris. The bastard just shoots me a wink as he makes his way back to his desk, Saint hot on his heels. They're together yet I got the vibe that both of them are interested in me.

Nick pushes off the wall and comes to stand directly in front of me. "Next time you want to get yourself off, don't." I flinch in shame. "Call one of us to help relieve that ache between those creamy thighs." I gasp in shock. Nick turns on his heel and marches over to his desk like he didn't just drop a fucking bomb on me.

Lord, please, bless my pussy with the strength to withstand these men. And, if it's not too much to ask, can you bless me with extra strength to handle the three extra men I am currently allowing into every part of my body? Kay, thanks!

CHAPTER TWELVE
SAINT

It's been three weeks since the first night we fucked Holly. Every night we follow her ass home or some times we change it up and beat her home and wait for her. But, regardless of how we get there, the night always ends the same—her passed out somewhere in her apartment from us fucking the shit out of her.

Chris and I are tired of the masks, especially after we walked in on her that day in the office. She hasn't said anything about it and nor have we.

Every day we come into work, we're forced to act like we have no idea what she tastes like, how her skin feels or what she sounds like when she comes and I hate it. I know she is attracted to us. I dare say the girl even has feelings for us. Every night we ask her if she's fucked her bosses yet and her answer is always the same, *not yet.*

We have two weeks until the office closes down for

the holidays and I should be thinking about this merger, but instead my head is full of thoughts of her! At the start she was just meant to be used, but the longer I watched her, saw how she lived, got to know her from afar, I knew I wouldn't be able to use her as leverage.

"Saint." I freeze at the entrance to the office building and whirl around to see my little brother running toward me. I narrow my eyes at the sight of him.

"What the hell do you want?" I snap when he comes to a stop a foot away.

He rolls his eyes. "My car broke down and my phone's dead."

I raise a brow. "And I should care?"

He scoffs. "Dude, can I just borrow your fucking phone to call someone. I can't leave my Bentley on the side of the road."

"You mean Dad's Bentley."

Anger flashes through his eyes. "Why do you always have to be such a dick?"

I scoff out a laugh. "Maybe because you tried to sink my company and then tried to sue me for an idea that I came up with and you claimed as yours. Hang on, how about the fact you lied and told Mom and Dad that I was the one that set their fucking house in Orlando on fire when it was you. Or how about the fact you crashed Mom's car, blamed me, and I got kicked out? Wait, if that isn't enough how about the fact you fucking reported my boyfriend to the cops and said he raped me!" I roar. I can feel the eyes of others passing by us but I don't care, this argument has been a long time coming and it's about time he learned that I will never forgive.

"Seriously? You hate me because I lied to Mom and Dad?"

I shake my head. "No, you dumbass. That shit I could have let go of. The fact you tried to sabotage my companies with Nick and Chris I could have dealt with, but I will never get over the fact you tried to send my boyfriend to prison. You were jealous I didn't fall on my face when Mom and Dad kicked me out and cut me off." I step into him so our chests are pressed against each other. "The only reason I am coming home for the holidays is because Dad is dying. If he wasn't, it would be like the past four years. You would be celebrating Christmas like an only child and Mom would photoshop me into the family picture."

He steps back and runs a hand through his hair. "Can I borrow your phone or not?" I scoff then toss the fucker my phone.

"Saint?" I turn away from my brother to see Nick and Chris walking toward me with tight expressions on their faces. Chris wraps an arm around my shoulders and pulls me in for a side hug. I relax into him. "What the fuck is he doing here?" Chris asks quietly.

"He said his car broke down and his phone is dead," I mutter.

"So?" Nick says.

I shoot him a *just let it go* look. He purses his lips and nods. "Are you okay?" I smile up at my boyfriend and nod. He places a chaste kiss on my lips.

"Here." I pull out of Chris's hold to face my brother. I grab my phone from him and tuck it into my coat pocket. "Look," he says, then sighs and shoves his hands into his coat pockets. "I lied, my car isn't broken down. I came here to try and work things out but..."

I recoil. "Why the fuck did you need my phone?" I snap.

He shrugs. "Looks like we aren't so different after all, brother." The cocky lilt to his voice puts me on edge.

"The fuck is that supposed to mean?" Chris grits out from behind me.

"Nothing at all. Dad will be pleased to know he has nothing to worry about with this merger now. See you soon, *brother*."

I haven't been able to shake the feeling my brother is up to something for days. I saw him Monday and it's Friday now. The meeting for the merger is next week and I have let my workload fall onto Holly, who is more up to date with things than I am.

She's the trump card.

"Hey, Saint?" I look across the conference room table to Holly. She looks worried.

"Yeah?"

"I'm not trying to overstep." I want to scoff, she has no idea I have been overstepping inside her every damn night for weeks. "But, are you okay?"

The fact she even noticed something was off with me has my chest tightening and warmth flowing through me. "Ah, yeah. I'm good. Just got a lot on my mind."

She nods and smiles but I can tell she doesn't believe me. "If you want to talk, I'm free... Well, I'm free during work hours." Her sheepish smile and the way she ducks her head down has me wanting to push her.

"So, does that mean if I asked you out for a drink tonight you would turn me down?" When she snaps her head up, shock is plastered across her face. I know for a fact she is trying to figure out a way to get out of it since she was ordered by us two weeks ago to head straight home after work every night.

She nibbles on her bottom lip. "I mean... I guess I could." Delight spurs to life inside me, knowing that I'll get to punish her ass tonight for disobeying our orders.

"Perfect, we'll head out straight after we finish here." I grab my phone off the table and shoot Nick and Chris a text.

Me - Snowflake just agreed to have drinks with me after work

My Boo - Is that right...

Me - Don't be jealous, baby, you're coming with me!

My Boo - You'll be sucking my dick on the car ride to her place

Nick - Her ass is getting fucking punished tonight! I want her chained and gagged. The filthy whore will be begging for mercy by the time we're done with her.

My cock is rock fucking hard and I still have two hours left on the clock before we're finished for the day!

Leaving work today I'm a nervous wreck.

I shouldn't be, but I can't help it.

Over the past few weeks I have spent every night with my masked men, trying new things, experimenting. It's been the best time of my life. I don't want it to end, but I'm also at the point where the secrecy is getting to me. My relationship with them isn't just casual anymore, I have feelings involved now and I'm terrified of that fact.

"You okay?" Saint asks as we enter the bar. I smile and nod but the pinched look on his face tells me he isn't buying what I'm selling. He leads us toward the back of the crowded bar. When I spot the guys waiting for us in the back, my smile isn't forced anymore. Nick and Chris grin back at me as I take a seat beside Nick.

"I didn't expect you to join us tonight," Nick says.

I shrug and shoot him a sultry look. "I live to

surprise." He nudges me with his shoulder, not only has my relationship with my masked men changed but so has the dynamic between me and my three bosses. It's not just work anymore. We laugh, joke and actually talk about mundane things. I feel like I know them better now—I mean, they have seen my pussy. I'm grateful for the fact that they haven't brought it up or poked fun at me. Nick's offer has been burning in the back of my mind every second of every fucking day.

There has been more than one occasion I have been tempted to take him up on his offer but it wouldn't be fair to him. Yes, I am fucking three guys and two of them are brothers but, Nick and Chris aren't them and I could never pick between them and Saint.

I want them all.

"So, are you ready for the merger?" I ask.

All three of them groan and suddenly the air in here feels thick with tension. I open my mouth to say sorry and change the subject but Saint answers. "I actually wanted to talk to you about that."

"Me?" I ask in shock.

He nods. "You've done more work on this than I have and I'm too behind to even catch up before the meeting next week. So, we talked about it and wanted to ask if you would be willing to sit in on the meeting and speak on my behalf?"

I turn to Chris and Nick to gauge their reactions to

find they are both nodding encouragingly. "Of course, we would compensate you for your time," Chris adds.

My mouth opens but no words escape, they already pay more than any assistant I know gets paid and here they are offering me more!

"Having you sit in on this meeting would really help us," Nick adds.

I mull over their words a second before I squeal and launch over at Nick and hug him. He laughs and returns my embrace. It feels so fucking good to be in his arms. I pull free and then round the table to hug both Chris and Saint and pray that being in their arms will feel like shit, but it doesn't.

By the time we finish up at the bar, I'm tipsy, horny and wishing I was climbing into the same car as my bosses and going home with them to fuck all night long.

I sit in the back of the car they ordered for me and scroll through my social media feed, but then a text message comes through from a random number.

Unknown - You're late!

Me - Who is this?

Unknown - One of the motherfuckers that's been making a home inside your pussy every night.

My eyes widen and I suck in a sharp breath. I know for a fact they have been watching me, they saw me playing with myself in the office, but I didn't think they had the power to get my cell number!

Me - I had a work thing, I'm sorry.

Unknown - You call going to a bar and trying to fuck your bosses a work thing?

I stupidly look around me and out the window to see if I can see anyone watching me, but it's dark and I see nothing but cars and headlights.

Me - I wasn't trying to fuck my bosses!

Unknown - That's another punishment added tonight for lying to us.

Me - Punishment?

Unknown - Tonight you will learn what it means to anger us. You belong to us, not just me!

A shiver works its way down my spine. I'm equal parts scared to find out what the punishment is and excited to see what they have in store for me. The drive ends quickly. I rush to get to my floor. As I stand in front of my front door, I take a moment to center myself. I know they are inside. I may not be able to see them but I can feel it.

I don't bother unlocking the door, knowing they would have left it open for me. I twist the handle and step inside. The lights are off and I don't reach to turn them on, knowing it will only piss them off. I lock the door behind me and drop my coat and purse to the floor.

"I'm here," I call out. When no one replies I scrunch my face in confusion. I carefully walk through the apartment, trying not to crash into anything. When I look down the hallway and see a red light coming from my bedroom, I make my way there.

As I enter the room, I spot the three of them leaning against the far wall with their masks and robes firmly in place. But, the thing that steals my attention is the sight of the bed.

"I told you that you would be punished," one of them says.

I shake my head and take a step back. "You run and we'll chase your fucking ass down and drag you back here," another adds, causing me to freeze on the spot.

They have handcuffs on each of the four posts of my bed, a spreader bar rests on the end and so does a fucking crop!

"Strip and get your ass on the fucking bed because we are about to own that ass and pussy by showing you why making us wait is never a fucking good idea," the guy on the right says as he steps forward.

CHAPTER FOURTEEN
CHRIS

Fear shines in her green eyes.

If you look close enough, you can see beneath that terror and find lust lurking there in the depths. She wants this, she's just too scared to admit she does because she's been trained by her ex to see this type of play as disgusting and taboo—but not with us. This is the type of shit we live for.

"You won't hurt me," she says more for herself than us. None of us bother to answer. It's ridiculous to punish her for hanging out with us, but the truth is... I'm jealous of the fact she was hanging out with us after work, knowing she would come home to be fucked by three random guys she doesn't even know.

She begins to undress and I'm like a moth to a flame, unable to look away from the sight of her creamy flesh. The lavender lingerie set she wears has my cock growing hard and need coursing through me. She wears skin-colored stockings, held up by a garter belt and she paired it with nude six-inch heels. She exhales and nods, then walks slowly toward the bed, her gaze flicking to the crop.

We wait for her to lay down and get settled before Nick and Saint move to secure her wrists and ankles with the cuffs. The sight of uncertainty on her face pisses me off, after everything we have done to her, *this* is the thing that scares her and not the fact we have been stalking her ass and breaking into her apartment every night!

"Relax, snowflake," Saint scolds. She closes her eyes, then inhales and exhales slowly, calming herself.

"This isn't like some horror movie where you are sick of me so you chain me up, then kill me and chop my body into little pieces, is it?" she asks.

I can't help but chuckle, then shake my head. "Nah, not tonight, baby. Where would the fun be in that?" I say as I move toward the bed and grab the spreader bar. She lifts her head and watches my every move as I slide it in place and secure it around her ankles. There really isn't any need for it, but we wanted to add it just to broaden her horizons when it comes to sex.

"We have another surprise for you," Nick says, then reaches into the pocket of his robe and retrieves the nipple clamps. Her eyes widen in surprise. Saint yanks the cups of her bra down, then the little fucker leans down and swipes his tongue across the hardened peak. She arches her back off the bed and moans. Before she can get into it, he pulls back and allows Nick to apply the clamps. When he's finished, Holly is already panting and trembling and we haven't even started yet.

Not willing to let them have all the fun, I reach out and grip her thong, then tear it off her. She gasps in shock. "Hope it wasn't a favorite," I say, just to be a prick, then stuff her ruined thong into my pocket. Her pussy is glistening with her arousal and my mouth waters at the sight, wanting to taste her but not yet.

I pull the tube of lube out of my other pocket and toss it onto the bed. She doesn't react to it, but when I pull the vibrator out she does.

"Oh," she breathes out. When Saint tosses the vibrating butt plug between her legs, she snaps her gaze to him. "What's that?"

"We've been going easy on you. Tonight, we are going to make you come so many times you'll be screaming for mercy, but we'll never grant it," Nick tells her.

Her eyes darken in outrage as she tugs against her restraints. "The fuck?" she snaps.

"No cock for you tonight, snowflake, but you will get to watch us fuck as part of your punishment." Her eyes fill with desire and the fight drains out of her instantly at the prospect of finally being able to watch us.

"I'll take whatever you give, just let me watch, please!" she begs. I smile behind my mask and refuse to answer. The guys take a step back as I begin lubing up her ass and the butt plug. I squirt onto my fingers and reach down to smear it around her ass and get her ready. When I push one finger inside her ass she cries out.

She was terrified at the idea of getting her ass fucked that first night in the office but now, she is fucking feigning for it and begs for us to fuck her ass. "Yes, fuck," she pants as I insert a second finger.

"On your knees," Nick snaps at Saint. Saint turns his back to Holly and does what he's told. Nick pushes Saint's mask to the top of his head. Holly pouts, hating she can't see Nick's cock disappearing inside Saint's mouth, but that's her problem, not mine. Once she is good and ready, I replace my fingers with the butt plug. A long drawn out moan comes from her the moment it's sheathed in her ass.

The sound of Saint choking on Nick's dick only heightens my need. I don't bother lubing the vibrator up, she's wet enough to take all nine inches of this bitch without a worry. I tune Nick's groans out as I slowly ease the vibrator inside her tight little cunt.

"Holy fuck," she shouts as I push it all the way inside her.

"Did I mention that the nipple clamps vibrate as well?" She tears her gaze from Nick and Saint to look up at me.

"Huh?" she breathes out. I don't bother with a response, instead I retrieve the remotes from my pocket and turn all three on. She jolts in shock a second before a moan slips out of her mouth. "Fuck."

I smirk as I move toward Nick and Saint. She lolls her head to the side, her eyes are glazed and her body is already trembling, mewls of pleasure tumbling free from her. I stare right at her as I part the lower half of my robe and expose my hard cock, pre-cum already glistening. I stand shoulder to shoulder with my brother. Saint releases Nick then wraps his hot mouth around my shaft. I tip my head back and growl my approval.

Tonight won't just be torture for her but us as well as we agreed she wouldn't be touching any of our dicks to teach her a lesson.

"You like watching my brother get his dick sucked?" Nick asks her as he begins to stroke himself. Her eyes are fixated on Saint as he bobs up and down on my dick.

"Oh, God, yes," she screams as her orgasm rips through her without mercy. Her whole body is shaking and her cries are like music to my ears as she comes undone at the seams. "Holy fuck!" she yells as I watch her cum leak out around the vibrator. I grip Saint's hair and yank him off my cock, then up the tempo on the vibrator, butt plug and nipple clamps. Holly's back bows off the bed and her restraints dig into her soft flesh as she screams.

I hand Nick the remotes as I move to the end of the bed, hunch over, then pull my robe up to expose my ass for Saint to fuck me while she watches.

CHAPTER FIFTEEN
HOLLY

It's too much!

Another orgasm barrels into me without warning. I'm not prepared for the intensity of it. I'm shaking my head side to side, unable to get the words out to beg them to stop. I lift my head and watch as the two guys down the bottom of the bed begin to fuck, their groans of pleasure are muted by my cries of agony. After-shocks are still coursing through me as I feel another orgasm building.

My nipples are pinched to the point of pain, but that small bite of displeasure only adds to the force of the climax. The single masked guy moves to stand at the top of the bed right in my eyeline, and despite the overwhelming need for this torture to stop, my mouth waters for a taste of him.

"I bet you want this cock, don't you?" I cry out as

he presses the button on the remote, making the butt plug switch its tempo. I slam my eyes closed and try to fight off the urge to come again. I can't fucking do it. "I warned you," he growls. Tears prick the backs of my eyes when I feel the orgasm crest. I snap my eyes open and look down at the two masked men fucking and that's what tips me over the edge.

I come with such a force that my screams are silent. I'm unable to make a single sound as my back arches and the cuffs dig into my soft skin as I tug against them. Tears leak out of the corners of my eyes. Who knew something so fucking beautiful could become something so cruel.

As the waves of pleasure release me from their strong hold and I find my voice again I say, "Stop this now!"

"I told you–" the one beside me tries to say but I cut him off.

"I don't care, I don't want this!" I yell, then begin sobbing. In a split second everything changes. The vibrators are yanked out of me, the clamps are removed, then the bar. When they finally release me from the cuffs, I tuck into a ball in the middle of the bed and cry. I don't know what the fuck happened but suddenly it went from excitement to... feeling broken and empty.

I don't know what the fuck is wrong with me!

"Nothing's wrong with you, snowflake." His

answer shocks me, I must have spoken out loud. I don't protest when I'm scooped up into one of their arms and held against them. Tears continue to fall and refuse to stop.

Is the sex great? Yes.

Everything about them is great, but it's missing intimacy. I get some people think being fucked is the most intimate thing you can do, but the truth is it's not. Being intimate with someone is allowing them to know you. To see you beneath the layers of bullshit you show the world. Cuddling, touching each other outside of the bedroom, holding hands and I don't have that. Yet, I fucking long for it.

These past few weeks have been amazing but my head is so fucked up. I'm behaving like a cheap whore. I lust after my bosses, who I'm pretty sure I'm close to really falling for, then every night, I come home to be fucked by complete strangers. I don't even know their names yet I have allowed them to do whatever the fuck they want to me.

"I'm... sorry," I stutter out.

"You have nothing to be sorry for," one of them says as he runs his fingers through my hair.

This.

This right here is what I want, the feeling of being wanted, loved and cared for. The three I want the most are out of my league and I have allowed myself to picture these guys as my bosses so I can live in a fake fantasy land.

After I fell asleep Friday night, they left. Saturday and Sunday they didn't come back and honestly, I'm grateful for that. I spent the whole weekend trying to sort my head out and think about what's best for me. When Monday morning rolled around I found I was excited to head into work and see the guys, but Sharon let me know the moment I stepped off the elevator that they would be out until Friday—the day of the meeting.

I have tried to call all three of them but none of them are answering, the only form of contact I have had from them was the note on my desk listing what I needed to get done and the time and place to meet them on Friday.

In the time that I have worked here, Nick has never left for a week. Sometimes he came in late or left early but never like this and something feels off.

Did I do something wrong at the bar?

By Wednesday, I am pissed. I haven't heard from any of them and not only that, I've had no contact from my masked men. I tried to text the number from Friday but none of my messages went through.

All this time alone isn't good for me. I've been left alone with my thoughts and now, all I want to do is see Nick, Saint and Chris and tell them the truth. I want them to see me as more than their assistant. I could be wrong and looking into things too much, but I swear, they feel the same way I do and are just too scared to admit it in case of a PR blow up from them banging their assistant.

I've been lumped with not only my own workload but the three of theirs as well. When I can't find the right document I'm looking for that we will need for Friday, I have no choice but to log onto Chris's computer to pull the file and share it with myself. Nick gave me a list of their passwords in case I would need them. I never thought I would, but clearly I was wrong.

As I scroll through his drive looking for the merger sales report I spot a file labeled...

Snowflake

Every instinct is telling me to log out and forget what I saw. My mind is trying to tell me that this is some coincidence and the fact it's snowing outside is the reason he would have a folder with that title, but the pit in my stomach and the lump in my throat are telling me to open it.

"Fuck it," I snarl into the empty room after a minute of debating with myself on what the fuck to do. The second the folder opens, my jaw hits the floor and pain explodes inside my chest at the sight of pictures, videos, copies of my bank statements.

I click open one of the documents and read over the contents. My stomach falls out of my ass. I scroll through all of them and click on one of the videos. Everything inside me freezes and bile rushes up my throat, forcing me to race into the bathroom to empty the contents of my stomach.

CHAPTER SIXTEEN

NICK

"Where the fuck is she?" Chris snaps from beside me.

I look down at my watch and grit my teeth, it's two minutes to ten and she was supposed to meet us here at nine-thirty for the meeting. The board and the others are in the conference room waiting for us.

"I don't know. Sharon said she was off sick yesterday and she's always on time—" I clamp my mouth shut when the elevator doors open to reveal Holly. My eyes are as wide as fucking saucers at the sight of her. Her long raven hair is curled and loose, her green eyes appear brighter, thanks to the makeup she wears. Her lips are painted a bright shade of red, but it's the sight of the white dress she wears that hugs her perfect curves that has me staring. It's cut low in the front to expose the swell of her tits. The skyscraper red heels she wears gives her a fucking edge.

She stalks toward the three of us with purpose. Her

eyes don't hold that same light look they normally do when she looks at us. She looks angry and ready to burn shit down. I expect her to stop and say hello to us, but instead she steps around Saint, pushes the door open and stalks into the room like she owns the fucking place.

"What the fuck..." Saint breathes out as he follows her inside. Chris and I are hot on his heels. Holly moves to the other end of the table and scoffs at the sight of her name tag that has her seated in the middle. She claims the seat at the head of the oval table, leaving me and Chris to sit on either side of her. Saint claims his place by my brother.

"What the hell are you doing here?" Chester bellows from his end of the table. I sneak a glance at Holly and frown when I see she isn't shocked to see her ex here. I glance over at Chris and Saint to see they both look just as perplexed as I am, but I'm not gonna call her on it in front of these fuckers.

Holly leans forward and staples her fingers, then rests her chin on top of them. "Oh, darling." I growl at her for calling him a pet name. "Are you intimidated by little ole me?" she taunts.

Chester's face turns red. His father places a hand on his shoulder, telling him to calm the fuck down without uttering a word. Chester Sr. looks like shit, it's clear to anyone with eyes that he only has a matter of weeks before he kicks the bucket. I shake my head, the fact he got his ass off his death bed to be here just shows how much of a cunt he really is.

"You two know each other?" Chester Sr. asks, his voice tinged with pain.

Holly smiles and nods, then shoots Chester a wink. "Sure do." I frown at her, I've never seen her act like this before.

"We more than know each other," that little cunt adds, making my brother, Saint and I snarl at him.

Holly waves us all off and smiles, but there is an evil tint to it which puts me on edge. This room is filled with our lawyers, Chester's team, and both of our board members. If she is about to have a breakdown, this is not the fucking place to do it! I reach out to touch her arm and she jerks away, shooting me a seething look that has me recoiling.

"I don't have much time to waste," Chester Sr. says, drawing our attention back to him. "This merger cannot go ahead," he says matter of factly

"Actually," Saint says, pulling the focus to him. "It can and it will. You're bankrupt and would rather cut your nose to spite your face than sign off on this, because you know it will help me."

Chester Sr.'s upper lip pulls back in a snarl. "I agreed to this meeting as a courtesy to your brother." I watch Holly's reaction to learning that Saint is Chester's brother, but she's a vault. There is no shock, anger or hurt, just a stoic look of indifference.

"Congratulations, you got your ass out of bed to

appease your dipshit of a son, just to piss the other one off that you hate. Sign the fucking papers, Dad, your legacy will be down the fucking drain if you don't and you and I both know that your favorite kid snorts too much coke and gambles every cent to his name." Both Chesters growl.

"This is my company and you aren't taking it from me, you fucking dick sucker!" Chester Jr. roars.

Anger swirls inside me at his insult. Saint shakes his head while Chris laughs and smacks his hand down on the table, making everyone jolt in fright.

"Oh, how long have you been saving that one, you little shit?" Chris says in a sarcastic tone, but both Saint and I know my twin is anything but calm right now. Not a lot bothers him in life, except fucking with me and his boyfriend. When Chester Jr. opens his mouth, Chris cuts him off before he can even utter a word. "You want to throw insults around, then you throw them at me, because the next time you come at my man with any shade, I will smash your fucking head through that wall."

Everyone around us begins to break out in shouts and protests, Holly, Saint, Chris and I all remain seated and calm. I'll back my brother till the day I die and the same goes for Saint. If you come for one of us, then you best be ready for the three of us to come back at you.

"Shut up!" Holly shouts. Everyone in the room looks at her in shock. "Sit the hell down, we're here to discuss business not your messy ass family dynamic." I bite the inside of my cheek to keep from smiling—her taking charge and commanding a room full of power has me hard for her.

"Watch your tone, sweetheart," her ex warns.

Holly rolls her eyes. "Or what?" she taunts.

Chester Sr. leans over and whispers in his son's ear. Whatever he says has the little cunt grinning like the Joker.

He clears his throat before he speaks. "My father and I would like for everyone to clear the room except for my brother, Holly and his friends." The others grumble their displeasure, but do as they were asked and exit the room. When we're alone, Saint's dipshit of a brother stands, then moves toward the door and clicks a button on the wall that has shutters rolling down to offer us some privacy. For what? No fucking idea.

The little shit snatches the remote off the table in front of his father and clicks a button that has the TV on the wall turning on.

"I'm gonna give you one last chance to drop this hostile takeover you are trying to disguise as a merger, or you leave me no choice but to resort to... *other* measures." The hysteria in his tone has my hackles raising. I look over to Saint for an indication if he knows what the fuck his shit stain of a brother is up to, but he just shakes his head.

Holly on the other hand, seems to be the only one in the know. She pushes her chair back enough so she can kick up her feet on the edge of the table and reclines back with a smile as she looks at the TV.

"No dice, darling, play whatever blackmail material you have so we can get this over with," she says with a cunning edge.

That little fucker smiles at her, the lustful look in his eyes has me wanting to smash his teeth out. "Oh, this is going to be so worth it," he mutters.

"Oh, I hope so because I am so excited," Holly adds smugly, making Chester sneer at her.

"You're gonna fucking regret this," he warns.

"Not as much as I regret you," she mutters beneath her breath, making the three of us laugh, but the moment Chester pushes play our laughter dies abruptly.

All three of the guys sit there with stunned expressions on their faces as they watch the video. Me, I'm just sitting here smiling. When Nick shoves his chair back and pounds his fist down on the table ready to lose his mind at Chester, I cut in before he gets the chance.

"Nick." Me calling his name draws his attention back to me, I keep my face blank of all emotion. "Sit your ass down. You're going to miss the best part, where Saint makes me squirt all over your desk while Chris is fucking him." The anger vanishes and his face drains of color at my words. I ignore Chris and Saint on my other side as I focus on the video. I can feel Chester and his father watching me intently, but pay them no mind. When the sound of my cries of pleasure bathe the room, I clap my hands and look at my ex. "Did you see how your brother made me come?" I don't give him a chance to answer. "I only ask because you've never been able to make me climax before but your brother has... multiple times on every surface of that office and my apartment. Oh, he even caught me fingering my pussy one day at work. Did you see that video?"

The room is so silent you could hear a pin drop. I look at each of the five guys with an unhinged smile on my face before finally settling back on my regret. I drop my feet to the floor and push to my feet. I lay my hands flat on the table and bend forward.

"If you plan to use that video to blackmail them into dropping this, then I'll be forced to counter your attack with one of my own." My tone is filled with warning, which he ignores.

"You don't have shit on me, sweetheart."

I laugh, but there's no humor to it. I feel Nick, Chris and Saint stand and flank me from behind. They know I know what they did, but they are choosing to play along with my game to save face.

I'll deal with them later.

"I have the audio of you telling me how you wanted to pull the plug on your father's machines, just so his death didn't drag out." Sr. splutters, but I'm not done. "Or how about the screenshots you sent of the PI you hired to tail your mother, only to find out she's having an affair with your dad's cousin. I also have the messages about you planning to use those against her so she would sign over her shares of the company. I also have the threats you sent me before I even knew Saint, about how you wanted to hire someone to run his car off the road so all your parents' assets would go to you and not be split."

Before Chester can utter a word, I turn around and face my lying ass bosses but my main focus is Saint who stands between the twins.

"If you had just told me the truth, I could have closed this merger in your favor months ago." He opens his mouth to reply but I hold up a hand, silencing him. "I've made a folder in the shared drive between the four of us and transferred ownership to you three. All the evidence you need to take your whole family down is in there. I also went a step further, I asked a friend of a friend to get me a copy of your fathers will. That's in there as well, but I think you should ask him about it, his answer may surprise you."

I spin around and face my ex and his father. I feel kind of bad for Chester Sr. but he brought this on himself.

"I don't appreciate being blackmailed or *used*." I hear the three behind me suck in a sharp inhale.

"Mr. North, none of this information has to go public. I have signed an NDA and added it to the file in the drive which Saint can send to you, but if this video is ever leaked to the press, I will spill all your family secrets and have no regrets, because I am that fucking petty." I look at my ex and scoff. "You really thought playing a sex tape of me would win you this?"

He scowls at me. "Fuck you."

I roll my eyes. "We've already established from that

film that your brother and the twins have been doing that every damn night. Do the right thing, Chester—"

"They broke into my house, hurt me and sent that text from my phone. I never wanted to break up!"

That is news to me and wasn't listed in the *snowflake* folder, but I don't show my surprise.

"Nothing you say will change the fact you just broadcasted my private life on tape and were planning to use it to hurt your own brother. Jesus Christ, Chester, you made Saint sound like a fucking monster. He's a good man. The three of them are! You chose to let your jealousy cause this rift between you and him, now you get to lay in the bed you made for yourself."

"Send my attorney the documents, I'll sign them," Chester Sr. says. I shoot him a small smile and nod.

"Thank you," I mutter, then walk out of there with my head held high. Now that the rush is wearing off I'm beginning to crumble and I need to get out of here before I break down. I won't let them see me fall apart. As I step inside the elevator, the three of them rush toward me. I press the door close button repeatedly, but Chris darts his arm out, stopping the doors from closing.

They all stand there panting and staring at me with varying looks of guilt, shock, pride and... love. I channel my inner bad bitch once more and force myself to stand tall and face them.

"Holly—'

"Don't you mean *snowflake?*" I hiss, cutting Nick off. He at least has the decency to look guilty.

"Can we explain?" Chris hedges.

"Nope. You had your chance to come clean, you didn't. So, here we are. Now, if you three could fuck off so I can get the fuck out of here, that would be great."

"Please, Holly, just let us explain," Saint pleads.

I laugh and shake my head, causing all of them to tense. "Get fucked. You really think I would stand here and hear you out after the three of you used me? Get fucking real, asshole."

"Those tapes were for us, we were never going to use them," Nick vows.

I shake my head in annoyance. "You don't fucking get it!" I shout, making them flinch. "Get the fuck away from me now, we're done." Chris drops his arm as he recoils.

"The fuck does that mean?" he snaps.

"It means I hope you like sucking your own cocks because I'm not doing it." The elevator doors begin to close and none of them move to stop them, but just before they close I call out, "Oh, and I quit." The second the doors close, my knees buckle and I drop to the ground gasping for air.

My chest feels like it's cracking open. The past two days I have been able to latch onto the anger and the rush of being able to serve them the smack down in that meeting, but now that it's all over, I have nothing left to keep me going except for the hurt and heartache.

A strangled sob escapes me as I reach the lobby. I pull myself to my feet and stumble out of the building, needing air. The moment the cool air hits me, I manage to suck in a full breath. Tears still trail down my cheeks and I start to walk. I have no idea where I'm going, all I know is I just need to get the fuck out of here and as far away from them as I can.

They're so stupid. The fact they thought I'm angry because of the masks is what pisses me off more. After all this time, I thought they knew me better than that but I was fucking wrong.

Dear Santa, if you forgive me for fucking your lookalikes, I promise not to sin... No, that's a lie but I promise not to sin as much!

CHAPTER EIGHTEEN

The victory of having my dad sign the papers doesn't feel as good as I thought it would. That's because she isn't here to celebrate with us. I did as she said and asked him about his will. To my surprise he told me he had left everything to me and not my little brother. Chester lost the fucking plot hearing that, but upon him explaining, I got it. I built something out of nothing and became someone he could respect. I showed him I wouldn't squander his empire, I would build on it and make it into something he would be proud of.

Our relationship will never be the same and I told him as much, money doesn't change the past.

I told him I wouldn't be coming home for the holidays, and the next time I would see him would be when he's in a box, then walked out of there feeling fucking lighter but not fulfilled. I'm empty inside and I hate it. When we arrive back at our office, a part of me is hoping that we'll see Holly, but when we enter the office and see her desk empty my stomach sinks.

"She's really gone," I mutter.

Chris claps me on the shoulder. "We'll figure it out."

I whirl around and glare at him. "How? We fucked up by lying to her and using her, just like Chester tried to do. Look how fucking well that ended for him! We did what you said and stayed away for the week to give her space after she broke down and all it did was cost us *her*!" I stab a hand through my hair and tug on the strands, we had her right in our grasp and then we fucked it all up.

"How the fuck did she know?" Nick wonders aloud. I pause and mull over his words, I'm trying to think if we said anything or did she notice Chris's tats, but that wouldn't explain how she knew everything else.

"The drive!" Chris blurts after minutes of silence. My and Nick's expressions mirror each other's.

"How did she get access to our drives?" I ask. Nick darts across the room to his computer and punches in his password, then brings up the drive the three of us share and checks the recent activity in the snowflake folder.

Wednesday two-thirty-two p.m.

. . .

"Fuck," I breathe out.

"She has our passwords. She must have needed something and then logged on and found the file," Chris says.

I nod my agreement as Nick begins to scroll through the folder. "Stop!" I snap when I see a video in there I have never seen before. "What's that?" I ask as I point to it. He clicks on it and pushes play. Holly's face fills the screen and the look of betrayal in her eyes cuts me to my fucking core.

If you're watching this, then you figured out how I know your dirty little secret. The pain that laces her words makes me feel like a piece of shit. I see the hurt in her eyes and it fucking kills me to know we are the reason for that look. *I guess I don't understand why you didn't just tell me the truth.*

Why all the lies?

You hired me because you knew I was dating Chester. You never thought I was good enough for the role. You tricked me into thinking you guys cared about me. You used me in the hopes I would be what you needed to bring Saint's brother and father down.

If you three had just told me from the start, I would have helped you. Instead you chose to believe the worst of me, thinking I would turn my back on Saint's cause.

Did you all laugh at me when you would go each

night, thinking about how funny it was to fuck me and then face me every day at work?

You stalking me and wearing the masks isn't even the part that hurts. I mean, I may not have known who you were but now that I do, part of me is happy that my dream came true and I got to know what each of you tasted like. I don't wonder how your skin feels or what it would be like to be at your mercy, because I got to experience it.

The part I can't get over is how you were going to use me. That's the part that fucking hurts the most. In case it wasn't clear, I quit. I cleared my desk out and Sharon will help you until you can find a new assistant. Don't bother trying to come to my apartment, I've already booked my flight and I don't plan on coming back for a long time.

I loved working with the three of you. Saint, you could always make me laugh and brighten any room you walked into. Chris, the way you listen to every word out of my mouth and pay close attention to my likes and dislikes is something I have never experienced before. Nick, we worked together for months and formed a bond like no other, you were there when I needed you the most and that will always mean something to me.

The three of you each gave me something I didn't know was missing from my life but it's all ruined because of your lies.

. . .

Tears shine in her eyes but she's too prideful to allow them to fall not wanting to allow us to see how deep her pain is. You can hear it in her tone how she is latching onto her anger so she doesn't have to deal with the heartache we have caused her.

When the video cuts out, we all just stand here silently staring at Nick's screen. My chest caves in and pain explodes inside me. I fucking love Chris more than anything. I love Nick as well. I may be dating his twin, but I love him just the same as his brother, but somewhere along the way I fell in love with someone else and judging by their reactions, they fell for her too. Now we're left here with nothing but the ghost of her memory.

Nick's the first to snap out of it. He pulls his phone out, then punches in a number and places it on speaker, then drops it on his desk before he starts typing on his computer.

"Nick?" the man on the other end says when he answers.

"Victor, I need a favor," Nick says curtly.

"What do you need?"

"I need you to find out what flight Holly Noelle is on, then send me the details." Chris and I glance at each other in shock, not knowing who the fuck this Victor is.

"Yeah, I'll get on to it, but Nick?"

"Yeah?"

"This is the last one for a while. I'm going off grid."

"Everything okay?" Nick asks.

"Yeah, just got a girl to hunt down," he says, then ends the call.

"Who the fuck was that?" I ask.

Nick peers back at me over his shoulder. "Victor is the president of the biggest MC in the state." My brows hit my hairline.

"How the fuck do you know him?" Chris presses.

Nick shrugs. "He wanted investment advice, and a year ago I helped him invest his money and tripled his ROI in three months. We've been friends ever since."

"You didn't think to mention to your buddies that you're friends with a biker gang president?" I snap.

Nick waves me off. "He's a good guy. Single dad, two sons and trying to build something for them. That's it. Now, as soon as he gets me her flight information, we're going."

I jerk in surprise. "What if it's too late?" Chris asks, the longing in his tone proves me right, they are in love with her.

"Then at least we know where she is, then we go there and find her ass."

CHAPTER NINETEEN
HOLLY

Colorado is stunning this time of year.

The mountains are covered in snow and the air is charged with the spirit of the holidays. I sit out front of the small quaint cafe, sipping my hot cocoa in the snow. I watch couples walk by and a pang of longing hits me. They all look so happy. Families pass by, smiling with their young children and I drop my gaze. I down the rest of my drink and head back to my hotel.

It's Christmas Eve and I don't feel like celebrating, this is my favorite time of year and they've ruined it for me!

The moment I enter the hotel lobby, I shiver as a blast of warmth hits me. I remove my gloves and stuff them in my pocket as I make my way to the elevators. When I step inside, I pull my phone and begin scrolling on my social media. I hear some others enter and keep my gaze down. When we begin to move, I sigh, time heals all wounds I guess.

"We gotta stop meeting like this, snowflake." I drop my phone in fright at the sound of Nick's voice. I snap my gaze up to see the three of them standing in front of me.

I've been trying to convince myself for days that they aren't as pretty as I remember, but it was all horse shit. They are fucking beautiful and they know it. They all look at me with so much love and longing in their eyes that a lump begins to form in my throat. I shake my head, unable to get any words out past the lump as tears fill my eyes.

When we come to a stop, I don't even check what floor we're on as I shove past them and escape. I make it two feet before an arm bands around my waist and I'm lifted off my feet and spun so I'm pressed against a chest. I keep my forehead pressed against his chest, I don't need to look up to know it's Chris holding me.

My tears roll down my cheeks unchecked, soaking his coat. He tugs the beanie from my head, then runs his fingers through my hair as the other two come to stand on either side of us.

"We can either have this conversation in the hallway, or you can let us into your room," Saint says softly. I debate my options, my mind is screaming for me to tell them to fuck off but my heart, that sucker is breaking in half. It wants them and is urging me to give into their request.

"Okay," I whisper, then pull out of Chris's hold, never looking up once as I blindly lead the way to my room. When I pull the card out to unlock the door, Nick snatches it, then pushes the door open and ushers me inside.

I head for the single chair in the corner of the room and sit down, crossing my legs under me. I can feel the three of them looking at me but I don't have the strength to face them, I needed more time so I could grow stronger before facing them again.

I'm pulled from my thoughts when Nick drops to his knees in front of me and cups my face between his hands, forcing me to meet his gaze. He swipes my never ending tears away with his thumbs.

"We fucked up and we know it," he says in a soft tone I have never heard him use before. "We kept those videos of us because we knew one day the truth would come out somehow and you would leave, then on the nights we missed you most, we would be able to rewatch them. We were never going to use those videos, Holly." I hear the truth in his words and I want to forgive them, but I can't.

"That's not why I left," I whisper.

Chris drops to his knees beside his brother and places his hand on my knee. The broken look in his blue eyes tugs at my heart strings. "We know why you left, baby."

My focus is drawn to Saint when drops down on Nick's other side. He reaches out and cups the back of my head. "We stalked you, that's true. At the start we had planned to use you against Chester, but the longer we watched, the harder we fell." A choked sound erupts from me. Nick's grip on my face tightens. "Chester was telling the truth when he said we were the ones who sent you that text."

"Why?" I ask brokenly.

"Because we couldn't stand to watch him with you," Nick says with dominance in his tone. "Yes, I hired you to keep you close, but as time went on, I forgot all about why I hired you because I fell in love with you." I gasp.

"All three of us want you, Holly. We love you and watching Chester with you was tearing us up inside, because he didn't deserve you, I know we pushed you too far that night. Seeing you breakdown destroyed something in each of us, that's why we stayed away from you that week because we couldn't face you knowing what we had done." Chris adds.

"Fuck, we don't deserve you either, but if you give us a second chance, I swear to you we will prove to you every single fucking day that we can be what you want. I'm so sorry for what we had planned to do and if we could take it back, we would," Saint implores.

"Snowflake, you may not have known who we were, but we knew exactly who you were and every single night we loved being with you, but it was during the day when we worked together that we fell head over heels in love because you are the total package."

Nick's words have me smiling and some of the tension easing inside.

"Why did you lie to me though? You could have come clean—"

Chris cuts me off. "We were fucking terrified of losing you. So many times we wanted to tell you it was us you were going home to, but in order to do that we would have to explain why we started following you and the truth scared the shit out of us."

"Will you please forgive us because we can't fucking keep living without you," Saint begs.

"Please, snowflake. We told you that you're ours but the truth is, we've been yours long before you even knew us," Chris adds, making my heart swell in my chest.

I look at Nick expectantly. The fucker smiles cockily like he knows they have already won me over. "Baby, I fell in love with you months ago and was just too chicken to make a move until my brother and Saint forced my hand." Hearing this big enigma of a man admit that he was scared of me has me laughing. I bat Nick's hands away and swipe away the remainder of my tears. The three of them remain kneeling, staring up at me, waiting for me to utter the words they long to hear.

I roll my eyes. "I guess I love you too. The three of you aren't easy to let go of or even forget, the way you make me feel safe, I need the intimacy from you, the connection of touch without the sex and being able to know the real you. I'm excited for the future and being able to get to know each of you on a deeper level because I can't picture my life without the three of you." Instantly their features shift. Gone are my soft, caring lovers who were begging for forgiveness. Their eyes are now filled with hunger and longing, and that single look speaks to my pussy and has her clamping down on air and growing wet.

"I'm so glad you made the right choice," Nick grits out as the three of them push to their feet, spin around and give me their backs. I balk at the assholes until they face me again, but this time the three of them are wearing their masks. The red LED masks are lit up, I used to find them ominous but now, all those masks do is make me wet. I snort out a laugh when I see Chris holding one of those giant candy canes in his hand.

"We were presumptuous and packed these in the chance you forgave us," Saint says.

I bite down on my lip and shrug. I push to my feet and relish the feeling of their attention on me. To further torture them for lying to me I decide to put on a little show of my own. I slowly walk toward the bed and skim the tips of my fingers along the comforter to draw this moment out. I keep my back to them as I grip my shirt and slowly pull it over my head.

Their groans only serve to heighten my desire, I slowly push my pants down making sure to bend right over so they get a good view of the thong lodged in my ass. They begin to mutter and curse beneath their breath but I'm not dragging this out. I slowly turn to face them wearing only my white lace bra and matching thong. Their heads dip to take in the sight of my pussy. I sit down on the edge of the bed and scoot back, resting back on my elbows. I keep my gaze on them as I open my legs and let them see what they have been missing.

"Snowflake." Nick grits out in a pained voice.

"I've been so lonely." I moan as I trail a hand down my body, gliding it over my tits and releasing a small moan. When I cup my pussy I arch my back and hiss.

"Let me take the ache away." Saint pleads as he steps forward but I shake my head and pin him with a hard look.

"No." I push my panties to the side and grip the string of my tampon, I ease it out of me then toss it over my shoulder.

"I'm so hard." Chris bites out.

"It feels so good." I breathe out as I slide a single finger through my folds. "I'm so wet." I tell them as I push the finger inside my tight little pussy.

"Fuck!" Nick snaps. I keep my eyes on them as I drag that finger out of me and bring it to my lips not giving a fuck it's coated in my blood, I groan as I lick it clean and relish the taste of my own need coating my tongue.

"We're sorry!" Saint shouts.

I release my finger and continue to torture them by making them watch me play with myself. "If you want this sweet ass pussy again you'll need to grovel and prove to me how much you want it, how much you missed it." I cry out when a wave of pleasure rolls through me. "Oh, fuck." The three of the, groan in agony and I fucking love it, serves them right for trying to play me!

"We'll show you with our mouths, cocks and fingers how much we missed you baby." Chris implores. My eyes are half lidded, I feel my orgasm brewing.

"I want to come so bad." I purr.

Nick growls and clenches his fists at his sides. "Fuck, we'll never lie again and hide shit from you, snowflake."

"Promise?" I pant as I sink a second finger inside my cunt.

"Yes!" The three of them yell.

A triumphant smirk touches my lips. "What have you got planned for me tonight?" I purr.

"First, we're going to cover this thing in some spice so you feel the burn you love so much, then we're putting it in your ass so Nick can eat it out," Chris announces, drawing a moan from me as I circle my clit.

"Tonight, we're going to show you what it's really like to be owned and loved by us. I promise you, snowflake, you will be begging for more," Nick promises.

"I'm on my period," I say, knowing they will fucking love it. I smirk when all three of them groan.

"Even fucking better," Saint says.

"Get the fuck up and get rid of those clothes, baby, I want to eat that bloody cunt out while my brother eats your ass," Chris demands.

I take it back, Santa, don't fucking forgive me because I plan on fucking sinning every night for the rest of my damned life!

THANK YOU!

THANK YOU!

I bet you want to play with your food now, don't you,
ya dirty girl!
Thank you for reading Naughty Or Nice.
I was so in love with the Sinners Welcome world I
couldn't let it go, so I made a spin off and I really hope
you liked the first book in this series.
I fucking had a blast writing this one, it was a damn
good time.
I hope you loved it just as much as I did, because if you
didn't, I might fucking cry!
I cannot thank you enough for reading *Naughty Or
Nice*, it means the world to me that you have taken a
chance on reading one of my books!

STALKER LINKS

Newsletter 🤍
Facebook 🤍
Reader's Group 🤍
Instagram 🤍
TikTok 🤍
Amazon 🤍
Website 🤍
Bookbub 🤍
Goodreads 🤍
Linktree 🤍

ACKNOWLEDGMENTS

Marcus, my bestie from another testie. You, my darling, are everything wrapped in a pretty red bow that I love watching get unwrapped by all the masked men we allow into our bedroom for research purposes. The way you take whatever I throw at you just shows how much of a real man you are, Daddy! Thank you for the *Figging* inspo, baby!

My demons, my little devils in the making. I love you both more than a fat kid loves cake and that's saying something... Mummy really loves cake! I hope you are proud of me but never read these books.

Leah, there should be a designer of the year award, my queen, because you would take that shit every year.

Sarah, I couldn't do any of this without you, babe. You keep our ship from sinking and make sure I keep on track. Without you I would be fucking lost. Plus, you are just as fucking sick in the head as I am, so that's why we rock at these novellas!

Lizz, you are the glue to this whole team. Without you we wouldn't be able to put out these books. Thank you my friend.

My alpha's, Debbie, Clare, Erin, Samantha

(number 2), Patti and Morgan, thank you all for being here and joining me on this fucked-up ride of smut and sinning. These books become what they are because of you all and for that I will be forever indebted to you.

My beta babes, Amber, Amanda, Nicole, Alex, Kira, Bonnie & Rizzo, saying thank you will never be enough. The amount of love and work you all put into these books means the world to me. I could never have asked for a better beta team.

My ARC army girls. You ladies are the best hype team in the world and I am truly thankful for all of you being here and coming along on this fucked-up ride as I try out new things and pump these books out.

My darling dark, delicious readers, your support over the years means more than you will ever know. Without all of you I wouldn't be able to live out my dream of bringing these characters to life. Thank you!

Sam xxx

Also By Samantha Barrett

Mafia Romance's

https://books.bookfunnel.com/mafiaseries

Secret Society/ Bully/ Masked Men

https://books.bookfunnel.com/dirtytemptation

Sinners Welcome (Pure Smut Novellas)

https://books.bookfunnel.com/sinnerswelcome

Samantha's Entire Backlist

https://books.bookfunnel.com/SamanthasBookverse

ABOUT THE AUTHOR

Samantha Barrett is originally from Auckland, New Zealand but now lives in Brisbane, Australia.

Sam writes all things dirty, dark and delicious with a side of twisted mind fuck.

She is a lover of all things red flags and an anti-hero is a must.